SIGNED, MATA HARI

A NOVEL

Yannick Murphy

LITTLE, BROWN AND COMPANY

New York   Boston   London

Little, Brown and Company
Hachette Book Group USA
237 Park Avenue, New York, NY 10017
Visit our Web site at www.HachetteBookGroupUSA.com

First Edition: November 2007

The characters and events in this book are fictitious.
Any similarity to real persons, living or dead, is coincidental
and not intended by the author.

Library of Congress Cataloging-in-Publication Data

Murphy, Yannick.
    Signed, Mata Hari : a novel / Yannick Murphy. — 1st ed.
        p. cm.
    ISBN-13: 978-0-316-11264-2
    ISBN-10: 0-316-11264-X
    1. Mata Hari, 1876–1917 — Fiction. 2. World War, 1914–1918 — Secret service —
Fiction. 3. Women spies — Fiction. I. Title.
    PS3563.U7635S57 2007
    813'.54—dc22   2006102966

                    10 9 8 7 6 5 4 3 2 1

                              Q-MART

                    Book design by Jo Anne Metsch

                Printed in the United States of America

For Non and Norman

SIGNED, MATA HARI

AMELAND

I CHEATED DEATH. I walked across the sea. When the tide was low I went over the furrowed sandbanks in my small bare feet. I skipped school one day and traveled to an island near my home called Ameland. I had heard stories, every child who lived in the Netherlands knew the stories, about the mud like quicksand and about the water like a great gray wall when the tide came in and how it could catch you and knock you down and pour into your mouth and drown you so that you couldn't ever return, no matter how hard you tried to climb out of the mud like quicksand and over the great gray wall. But I returned. I went back to the nuns, who had been tolling bells, looking for me. When they found me they showed me their palms, raw from pulling the bell's rope, and they took me to the headmistress for punishment. Walking to her chambers I whispered proudly into the black folds of their habits. I have walked across the sea. Later my whispers came out as the nuns knelt for Mass, released like cold air once trapped in a cellar, now mixing with their prayers.

I KNEW my walk at low tide to the island of Ameland would always be with me. I was to walk it years later, again and again, in bed with men who snored beside me, a meaty arm of theirs across my chest. In the hot, sweaty jungles of Java I walked the wet sand to Ameland and did not always smell the smell of the lotus growing out my window, but instead I smelled the cold salt spray of the ocean of my homeland. I walked my walk to Ameland most often in the prison of Saint-Lazare, where every stone on the floor of my cell held a trip for me across the darkened sand. When I walked back, I turned around and looked over my shoulder to watch the sea advancing. Try and catch me, I said out loud, and what answered back was the sky, at first in low rumbles, then louder as thunder rolled closer. But it never did catch me, and I outran the tide and lived.

———

FIRST THERE is flour, mother said in the kitchen. Then the eggs. With the flour on her hands, puffing up along her arms, she was already becoming a ghost.

The cake she made was for my birthday. My father said that in a country called Mexico the birthday child's face is pushed into the cake. For good luck and a long life, he said.

Not in this country, my mother said, and she slid the cake away from me so that I would not push my face into her frosting, spread with a spoon so that it looked like small cuppy waves, curved tips held suspended in a gentle roll.

Father said, Next birthday when you are fifteen, Margaretha, you can do it.

I was given weekly horseback riding lessons for my birthday.

After the lessons I went to Father's store.

One time he showed me a hat.

Touch it, he said. He rubbed the soft felt against my cheek.

Think of the animal that died so that this hat could be made from its fur, he said.

I pushed the hat away. I wanted to think of all the men who would wear the hat and the parties they would wear it to.

Father put the hat in the window to display it, but I knew that in an hour or so he would take it down and replace it with another hat from a shelf inside the store. By doing this, he kept the colors of the hats from fading in the sun.

Father was not there for my next birthday. He closed up his shop. He took down all the hats and sold them at reduction and held the cash in his hand and licked his fingertips to count without making a mistake. I sat in the storefront window. The sun beat down through the glass and I now knew how quickly the hats could fade and lose their color and I thought how funny that was because everyone had always told me to stay out of the sun, saying it would make my olive skin darker.

After he was gone, all that was left of him was a flowered vest he once wore that hung in the closet. The vest was stretched around the waist, where the girth of him had pushed against the cloth. Mother never put anything else in the closet, and if I opened the door quickly, the breeze would set the flowered vest in motion on the wooden hanger.

He gave us no address. He left saying he would come for us after he found a job in the south.

Mother cried at night. There were holes in the walls, large patches where the paint was peeling and the plaster was crumbling. I thought her cries would enter the holes and stay forever in the house, trapped and ricocheting behind our walls. I tried to drown out the cries by pounding out songs on the keys of the piano, but all that happened was the paint peeled even more, the plaster crumbled to the floor and left small white piles like those inside a sand timer, marking hours that could not be turned upside down.

I found mother dead in the kitchen. The white flour was on her apron. It was up her arms. It was between the laces of her boots. It was in her mouth. The doctor said she died from an infection in her lungs. I thought she died from breathing in the flour. From the inside out, it turned her into a ghost. I never went into that kitchen again. The kitchen can kill you, I thought. I closed my eyes and was walking across the sea. Each time I remembered it, it was as if I were more there than the first time. I noticed more things. The white sand crabs burrowing beside my feet. The water coming in, the bubbles springing up from beneath me, filling in between my toes, creeping up the hem of my silk skirt.

LET THEM HEAR

SHE THOUGHT the nun at the prison of Saint-Lazare held her whispers in her robes, too. She knelt down and felt the cold of the silver cross hanging from the nun's waist against her cheek as she spoke the same words she spoke as a child: I have walked across the sea.

Do you pray for your soul? asked the nun.

No, she answered. She wanted her words to be released throughout the prison as the nun walked away. Let the rats hear them as they run through the dark, wet walls. Let the cooks hear them while thinning soup in the kitchen. Let Bouchardon the lawyer hear them as he taps his pencil on his pad, thinking of questions to ask and trap her in a life she did not lead. I have walked across the sea, she said. I will live.

EARTHWORMS

THE THING ABOUT CHILDREN is that I never understood them. It took one or two tries before I knew what they were saying. They'd have to point. Speak up, I'd say. It was because their mouths were so small that they could not open them enough to say words I could understand. I told my godfather this, but he said their cheeks are like apples, and their hair is made of sunshine, and that, really, I had no choice and he didn't have the money to keep me fed and clothed. So he sent me to teach at a school.

The children's cheeks were pale and their hair slick with grease that always made the little girls look as if they'd braided their hair right after washing it and the water never dried and it made the boys look as if they'd dunked their heads in the wash water only moments before.

You must learn to rap their knuckles, Heer Wybrandus said. He gave me a ruler for the job the first day I started. This is all you'll need, he said.

Ink? Pens? Paper? I said.

He laughed. Yes, those too, he said, and he licked his lips, which were just two straight lines that looked like earthworms, one on top of the other.

Later he kissed me with those lips, and it was easier thinking of them as earthworms than thinking they were Heer Wybrandus's lips.

The children did not learn from me. I wrote letters on the board, and they stared out the window cawing back to the black birds or pulling at one another's slick hair.

I told you to rap their knuckles, Heer Wybrandus said into my ear. Afterward, in class, I put a loose strand of my hair behind my ear, and my ear and my hair felt wet from Heer Wybrandus's mouth.

He called my breasts champagne cups because they were so small and he said he had to drink from them. He wet his finger with his tongue, then traced my nipple and covered it with his mouth.

Salud, he said.

A VISIT FROM THE DOCTOR

In Saint-Lazare she said she'd like to see the doctor. He came in wearing a white coat. The rubber on his stethoscope looked old and cracked in places.

Your gown, Dr. Bizard said. She did not lower it over her shoulders.

Do it through the gown, she said.

I cannot hear your heart as well through the cloth, he said.

It's not my heart that needs listening to, she said. He smiled. He took the stethoscope and set it on the cot covered with a wool blanket, then leaned back against the chair. His eyes were blue and she thought how that should have been the color of the sky that day she walked across the sea to Ameland.

She'd like to have told him everything, but his blue eyes looked as though they knew it already. Instead she danced for him, for his eyes, just to see if the blue would change by the light of her dancing.

I had heard you were a great dancer, he said, and now I know it's true. Afterward he clapped a steady clap of applause, and she wished her heart would follow its rhythm instead of pounding the way it did, as if it could pound its way out of her chest.

LESSONS

THE CHILDREN IN CLASS weren't learning anything, but I was. Heer Wybrandus taught me about being a woman.

Shouldn't I be learning this from other women? I asked him.

No, he said. Other women won't teach you anything. To learn what it is to be a woman, your teacher must be a man.

He told me what my monthly bleeding meant. He said it was my best friend because it told me when not to have coitus if I wanted to avoid becoming pregnant.

Other women call it the curse, he said, and that is entirely wrong. They should call it the gift instead.

When he was not telling me things, he was showing me. He would touch me with his fingers and then he would make me use my own fingers and explore myself as well so that I would know how it should be done. He gave me homework.

Practice in your room tonight, he said. His fingers looked like stubby sausages compared to mine, which looked to me like the ivory blades of finely carved letter openers, and I wondered if I would cut myself with them. After I did it I realized that the only thing that could really hurt me was the bed I slept in whose middle sank down into a pit. Every time I lay in it, the bed seemed intent on folding me in half.

*　　*　　*

HEER WYBRANDUS liked for me to sit on his lap. I could feel his pulse beating between his legs, and he would reposition me sometimes or move me from side to side, saying as he did that I was making him grow, and he said, Can't you feel how large I am? but I shook my head. He was small and what I felt the most through my dress was his warmth and the tap-tap-tap against me of his beating pulse.

By the river on a grass field on a blanket his wife had embroidered around the edges, I would sit on him, and when he asked me again if I could feel how large he was and I shook my head he pushed me off and so I began to fold up the embroidered blanket and Heer Wybrandus grabbed it from me in the middle of my folding and bunched it into a ball and then ran toward the riverbank and sent it flying over the tall grass and cattails, where it landed in the river and unfolded slowly in the current.

On the walk back to the school, he said it was my fault that I could not feel how large he had grown between his legs and that I had not done my homework well, I had not bothered to learn the lesson of being a woman yet.

I stopped listening to him. I thought again about my walk across the sea. When the tide goes out across the flats of Ameland, flocks of terns come to feed on the muddy sea bottom. When I walked across the sea the terns wheeled down in front of me and I saw seals lolling on the sandbanks. I thought that when the water returned, the terns and seals would be safe. They would fly away or swim. But in my silk skirt, whose hem was getting salt-stained and heavy, I would drown. My skirt would keep me down. I could have taken the skirt off. There was no one else to see me on the flats that day. But I didn't. I think I liked knowing that the odds were against me.

IF YOU WANT TO BE A SPY

I T HELPS to be fluent in a number of languages if you want to become a spy. I spoke Dutch, German, Spanish, French, and even Malay. If you have a studious mind, this helps you become a spy. If you do not have a studious mind, this too helps, because who would suspect you, being ignorant of how to break a code, of knowing how to concoct invisible ink from a number of vials? Anything helps if you want to become a spy, because everyone wants to believe you are a spy.

Sit with your left leg crossed over your right in a restaurant, then uncross them, then cross them again with your right leg over your left leg, then voilà, you are a spy and the waiter has reported you to the authorities and you all the while are just wondering why the coffee is taking forever to come to your table.

If you read the paper, you can be a spy too. You can tell your German lover something you read in the paper or something the hairdresser told you while you were having your hair dyed, and it will become a secret no one else knew and you are aiding and abetting the enemy. You could vow not to talk to Germans, but that too is suspicious because you always used to talk with them.

You could have spent ten years of your life being a famous

exotic Eastern dancer and that gets hardly a mention on the lines of the pad of paper Bouchardon is writing and tapping his pencil on, because really your whole life, from the day you walked across the sea to Ameland, you were a spy. The terns, the seals, the couch grass and sea rocket and thrift and seaweed beneath your feet whispered secrets that flew to you in the wind before a thunderstorm, secrets you relayed back to the nuns (they too can be spies), and you are guilty and the firing squad is dismantling their guns, cleaning their barrels, oiling the working parts, getting ready for when you are placed in their line of fire. And how do you convince Bouchardon you did not give secrets to the Germans when Bouchardon is so busy at the windowpane, drumming his fingers against it, some kind of nervous habit that sounds like his own secret code, telling everyone, the dirty gray pigeons shitting on the ledge even, that you are guilty to the marrow of your bones.

THE RIGHT HEIGHT
FOR A MAN

Heer Wybrandus hung his head low and did not look up at me when he told me I had to leave the school.

My wife, the town, they know about us, he said, as if speaking to his massive belly. And they know you are only seventeen.

I gave him back the ruler he had given me to rap the children's knuckles. I had never used it except to draw lines.

I went to live with my uncle in The Hague. I did the household chores. I bought the bread and vegetables and meat at market. I washed the long windows while standing on chairs needle-pointed with designs of flower bouquets. I scrubbed the tiled bathrooms and smoothed the linens over the beds and fluffed the down feather pillows. I cooked the meals, and this was the part I did not like, because I had to be in the kitchen and I knew from experience that the kitchen could kill you.

You're too tall for a man, Uncle told me once.

I'm a woman, I said.

Yes, of course. What I mean, he said, is that you'll have difficulty finding a husband.

I thought about my walk across the sea to Ameland then and

how I lived to tell the tale. Out loud, I said, I have walked across the sea.

What was that you said, dear niece? Uncle said.

I'll start dinner, I said.

WISH YOU WERE HERE

So it was that the spaces in between the stone walls of her cell held the cries of other prisoners and she put her ear up against the cracks and told the nun she could hear them. Then she moved her cot away from the wall and slept in the middle of the cell.

Sticking out from the wall was a single gas flame for light. It flickered as if there were a constant wind on it, threatening to blow it out. She asked for pen and paper. Sister Leonide brought them to her.

Are you going to write your Russian fiancé? she asked.

I will write two letters, she answered. One to the Dutch consulate asking again if they can release me from this prison. The other is a letter for my daughter.

What will you say in the letter to your daughter? asked Sister Leonide.

I don't know. I could tell her that I'm having a wonderful time here.

Sister Leonide shook her head.

THROUGH A WATER DROPLET

As IF my uncle knew it was the flour I least of all wanted to cook with, he began to ask for homemade biscuits every day. With a metal cup I scooped up the flour from a jar and poured it into a bowl. I added butter to the flour and with two knives I cut the butter so that it would mix with the flour. I thought I had done all right. I thought I had done a good job not getting the flour on me, but as it turned out I was wrong. I first saw it on my eyelashes. In the tiled bathroom I had scrubbed on my hands and knees earlier in the day, in the mirror I had washed and wiped dry and streak-free with yesterday's newspaper, I saw the first signs of my becoming a ghost.

Niece, dear, would you empty out the trash while you're in there, Uncle said on the other side of the bathroom door.

The newspaper I had dried the mirrors with was in the trash. It was crumpled and wet, but still I could read the classified ad. *Captain of the Army of the Indies, on leave in Holland, seeks a suitable wife* . . . I shook the page dry, letting drops of water slide across the type, magnifying the word *wife.*

Niece, is there something burning in the oven?

I balled up the classifieds and stuffed them inside the cup of my brassiere, and then as an afterthought, to avoid looking lopsided, I crumpled up the headlines too and stuffed them into the other cup of my brassiere. Then I opened the door and ran past my uncle to the kitchen. The biscuits were black on top. I cut the tops off and served them anyway.

Uncle didn't notice. What's different about you today, niece? You're looking lovely, he said while staring at the new size of my breasts.

I ANSWERED Rudolph MacLeod's ad that evening. In the envelope I also included a picture of myself that I thought made me look a little older, a little more of the marrying age.

I liked the way the crumpled newspaper in my brassiere made my breasts seem larger, but I did not like how the newsprint blackened my skin and how the newspaper's crumpled edges dug into my flesh and made me want to scratch. I pulled silk stockings from my drawer and they were soft against my skin and I stuffed my brassiere with those instead when I first met Rudolph MacLeod.

There was something about a man in uniform that I liked. Maybe it was that it made him look rigid and I liked thinking how I would be the one to undo his brass buttons and throw back his lapels and make the jacket he wore hang half off his shoulders and lose its shape and crease where the tailor who sewed it never meant it to as I straddled him in a chair or as he lay in bed. Then, in the morning, he would stand up naked, slightly stooped from fatigue, a hangover playing behind his eyes, and he would fit himself back into his uniform, and all the buttons would be buttoned in the right place and the lapels would be straightened, and once again he would be an officer standing tall before me.

MacLeod was balding, and where there was hair at his

temples it was graying. But he was in good shape, and did not sport the belly that Heer Wybrandus sported, and when I sat on his lap I could feel much more than just the beating of his pulse.

I'm getting married, I told Uncle.

What a relief that there is someone who wants you, Uncle answered.

THROUGH A TINY PORTHOLE

I HADN'T PLANNED on it so early, a child to raise. I could think only of the children at Heer Wybrandus's who were my pupils and who never listened to me when I taught a lesson. But MacLeod had come back from a night on the town and he already smelled like another woman mixed with his own smell when he decided to enter me. I counted the days from the start of my last period, splaying my hand on the sheet as I ticked them off with my fingers, while he forced himself into me. It was the wrong time to have coitus. Heer Wybrandus had taught me that.

I knew from nights before that if I had tried to push my husband off he would just push himself deeper into me, making it hurt, or he would hit me and in the morning my cheek or my eye would be swollen and I'd have to walk to market with a scarf covering my face, even on a hot, sunny day.

The nights he stayed out with other women grew in number and in proportion, I thought, with the size of my expanding belly. My belly button started to protrude and it stuck out like a third eye and I wondered if it was the place my unborn child first saw the world from. Did the unborn child peek from its small porthole into the room where MacLeod was busy picking up an empty decanter and throwing it against the wall so it rained down crystal?

Damn it, he said. Can't you remember to keep it filled! he yelled.

The baby kicked. It jabbed up under my rib.

I'll try to remember, I said. But then I added, If you try to remember not to empty it so often.

What's that you said? he yelled, and he came for me and I went to Ameland in my thoughts again while I heard the joints in my neck crack like knuckles cracking as he dealt me the first blow.

AT FIRST the darkness over the sandbanks reminded me of the time after the volcano of Krakatoa in Indonesia had erupted, sending smoke and ash into the atmosphere. The skies were dark from the ash that drifted across the world. My father closed shop early in the evenings that followed. We ate dinner early and went to bed early. Days went by and then the darkness lifted, but my father still closed the shop early. He would come home and he would carry me outside on his shoulders. We would walk to the hill behind our house and stand and watch the sunset. The sunsets after the eruptions were all beautiful. They were purple and gold and red and streaked. In places they looked like bright wads of cotton that had been pulled at from the sides and stretched across the sky. But it had been years since the eruption that day I walked across the sea. The darkness did not come from ash and smoke in a distant land. It just came from the clouds gathering for the usual summer storm over a waterless sea.

My father came to my wedding and that is the last time I saw him before he died, but really all I saw of him was the back of him walking away. I was told he was at the wedding and then after I took my vows I ran down the street to see if I could catch him. I saw his back walking up the hill. MacLeod chased me and grabbed me and told me to come back inside, saying that my father was walking away because I wasn't marrying into money. But there was a gorgeous sunset that day. He must have wanted to see it. He must have wanted to go to the top of a hill the way we used to when I was a girl. That's why he left early, I told MacLeod. He just wanted to look at the sky.

I RODE a horse when I was pregnant. I wore MacLeod's pants and since I could not button them over my belly I sewed them with one loose wide stitch at the waist so they would not fall.

The pants did fall in a fast trot on a long stretch of trail clover-lined and carpeted with cherry leaves. When I returned to the stable, MacLeod was there. The neighbor had told him she had seen me leaving the house with my riding boots on.

MacLeod accused me of coming to the stable because, he said, I wanted to make love to the stable boy. The stable boy hid in a stall, peeking from behind a wooden wall chewed up by a nervous horse so that the wood was now splintered and raw. I laughed at MacLeod, and the horse that I had just ridden jerked back its head, and its black mane bounced on its neck, shiny with sweat.

MacLeod walked me home and he held my arm hard as we walked through the streets and he tipped his hat to passersby and with my hand in the shape of a fist I held onto the waist of my pants so they would not fall down to my ankles.

MacLeod felt the need to watch over me as if I were a child. Before he left the house he would make sure I was not cooking something in the oven that I would accidentally forget about and somehow set the place on fire. At a party for officers he wanted to take me home early one night. The other officers were dancing with me, one right after the other, and he wanted to protect me from them, as if I were the daughter he did not yet have. Their hands slid down the length of my back, their pinky fingers turned in the direction of my buttocks, poised to reach down like a divining rod that could not help itself in the presence of water. He watched me grow, not in height, but in awareness. At first I did not know the men were looking at me, and then I knew they were looking at me, and then I knew I wanted them to look at me.

SNAKES ON THE PILLOW

IN THE MORNINGS she had coffee. Sister Leonide would bring it to her and tell her the weather. The degree. The high and the low. She would drink it while still under the wool blanket and propped up on her side. Sister Leonide would ask her if she wanted to join her in morning prayer and she would shake her head.

You say it without me, she would say. Before she finished all of her coffee, she would make sure to leave some in the cup so that she could see her reflection in it when she combed her hair. She could not tell very well from the reflection how badly her hair was turning gray, but she could tell from the pillow she slept on at night. She would notice hairs that were half dyed black and half gray that had fallen out of her head in her sleep as she turned her head back and forth on the pillow. They lay in S-shaped curves on the pillowcase like snakes and she told Sister Leonide that, being like snakes that could rise up and bite, they were good luck and she told about how when she lived in Indonesia the old people would have been interested in her S-shaped gray-and-black hairs and they would have told her all the snake stories they knew and showed her their snake tattoos, faded now and hard to see within the lines of their loose, hanging skin.

A GOOD FATHER

THE MOMENT my son was born, MacLeod scooped him from the midwife's arms and carried him down to the corner to the Café Americain. I imagined he showed the other officers his boy, and they passed MacLeod a whisky, and as he drank while smiling, yellow drops of it fell from his mouth, quickly soaking into my boy's white blanket.

I lay in bed, waiting for him to bring me back my son. MacLeod was gone such a long time I thought maybe he had left with my son for good and now all I would have would be the pain from the stitches between my legs and two rock-hard breasts that had already begun to leak milk, like water from a stone.

MacLeod was not the father I thought he would be. He came back and was there beside his new son all night. He leaned over and peered at my boy when my boy slept and he was worried by the small animal noises my boy made in his sleep. He shook me awake when my boy woke and made sure he was drinking enough and that all of my nipple was correctly inside his mouth. While I nursed my boy, MacLeod laid his hand on the mattress of the crib so that the space there would be kept warm for when he was put back to sleep. MacLeod told me that I was fastening the pins on my boy's diaper too tightly, and he showed me how I should do it so as not to hurt my boy's soft skin. Then he named my boy Norman, after his father, and I felt that it was just the start of my boy, my Norm, being taken away from me.

When MacLeod said his long leave was over and that we would now have to go to Indonesia, the sound of the name floated out of his mouth and at the same time he said it I thought I smelled the sweet smell of spice mixed with a nut smell, a damp smell, a blooming flower smell, and I hurried to my Norman and picked him up and whispered *Indonesia* into his ear and he looked up at me and laughed and clapped, as if the word itself was the start of a nursery rhyme song he had heard countless times before and knew that I would sing to him again.

THE DAY we left on the SS *Prinses Amalia,* MacLeod put his finger in his mouth and held it up to the sky, telling Norman that was the way to tell which direction the wind was coming from. The wind was from the east. That night in our cabin, with Norman asleep, MacLeod wanted me to stay awake and listen to him.

There were scorpions and bugs and snakes and monkeys I should know about. There were things in Java that hung from the trees that could strangle Norman and there were roots on the ground in angry, tangled masses that could trip him. There was rain that could drown Norman if he stood out in it too long. There were eruptions from volcanoes whose ash could choke him. Why are you smiling? MacLeod asked me. He could see my face in the light of the moon that came in through our window.

I can't wait to be there, I said. I feel as if my whole life I've just been waiting to live there and now the time has finally come.

The damn humidity there makes my bones ache and the crack in my ass chafe, he said. I laughed when he said it and then he told me to hush, that Norman was sleeping, so I covered my mouth because I could not stop from laughing. Then MacLeod said he couldn't sleep and he sat up in the narrow bed we shared and he lit his pipe and I watched the smoke rise toward the ceiling of our cabin and blanket us like some sort of mist-covered sky. It was under the swirl of his pipe smoke that I decided to make love to him. Java was going to be a new beginning for us. I wanted it to start out right.

A HAIR

SHE WAS ALLOWED into the yard only by herself. The other women prisoners were let out before her. She was kept separate, Bouchardon said, because the other women might have ripped out her hair and clawed her eyes if they saw her. Spies were worse than whores or thieves or baby killers, she was told. There wasn't anything in the yard. It was just more stone around her. She looked for signs of the other women prisoners who had walked in the yard earlier in the day. If it was raining, she could sometimes see a footprint on the stone floor, though it would fade quickly, new raindrops covering it. But she wanted to walk in the footprint herself, to feel what it felt like to walk the same steps another woman had walked.

Occasionally, there was a strand of hair on the walls stuck to the rough surface of a stone. It would waver in the wind and she watched it and then pulled it from the wall and held her hand high and let the wind take it over the stone wall and carry it somewhere else. After a quarter of an hour, she had to go back inside to her cell. When she entered it she would sit on her cot and close her eyes. The wall, the sky, a bird, whatever she had seen out in the yard was etched in silver under her eyelids and she watched it for as long as she could until the image blurred and blackness took its place.

THE OGRE

AT THE COAST, the beaches were windswept and smooth. The sand was white and fine and nothing like the dark sandbanks I had walked across to Ameland. We walked inland for the first time toward our new home and saw sparkling white waterfalls flowing down from shallow swamps and broad estuaries. Under our feet white and pink blooms covered the sandy trail and gnarled trees edged along the boiling ocean where huge waves rolled and crashed, rolled and crashed. Never take Norman here, MacLeod said, and we kept going.

From across the savanna, tinted gold and orange from a new sunrise, black banteng bulls snorted powerfully and left a trail of hoof marks along the rims of muddy pools where they had wallowed. Away from the bulls, fawn-colored females grazed peacefully and their young calves stood beneath them, shyly peeking out from behind their mothers' legs at the mist clinging low to the ground and slowly burning off in the increasing heat of the day.

Crisscrossing in front of the banteng bulls were small groups of rusa deer and wild pigs and in the trees pied and wreathed hornbills skittered back and forth and then suddenly they took flight with a great beating of their wings, which made us jump.

The wild pigs could kill a small boy easily, MacLeod said while I watched eagles and hawks soar above us, their eyes keen on squirrels or mice afoot on the ground where dry twigs and fallen leaves lay, lit by shafts of sunlight. MacLeod covered his ears. He did not like the constant sound of the insects buzzing and chirring and thrumming that like the sound of the crashing waves at the shoreline did not ever stop.

We traveled a thin trail woven with vines, swollen as thick as MacLeod's arms, and the vines' blossoms had yellow and red hues that were radiant among all the green. A purple flower with a purple stem was picked by the Javanese men carrying our water. MacLeod said the locals used the flower as an aphrodisiac and also to make wax for candles. Don't touch it, it might be poisonous, he said. In fact, don't pick anything that grows, and eat only fruit that you'll see served at the restaurant in the commissary.

Threaded up in high branches, orchids grew, and the sodden earth was dark and rich, pressed gently into leaf-covered hills. It was tight and humid among the foliage, and MacLeod cursed and said stop to the Javanese men carrying our water and took a long drink from the skins they carried while I looked up and listened to the riot of noise coming from what MacLeod said were silver leaf monkeys and gibbons and long-tailed macaques. A mynah bird stared at us from a branch and then flew off and a kingfisher soon took its place. MacLeod pointed out a footprint and then pointed to the wooded shadows. Jungle cat, he said, spotted and black leopards and civets abound here, he said. They'll attack a human without a moment's hesitation, he said, especially a young boy. Isn't that right, Tekul? he said to one of the Javanese men holding our water. Tekul nodded and smiled.

Yes, sir, he said, and then he handed MacLeod the skin of water again.

No, I'm finished with the goddamned water, you idiot, he said. The cats, I'm talking about the cats, he said. They'll kill you, won't they? Tell my wife how they'll kill you in an instant, MacLeod said.

Tekul nodded again. Yes, ma'am, he said. If you ever see a cat, you run, he said.

Have you ever seen one? I asked him.

No, no one ever sees the cats, he said. They see you first, they run first, Tekul said.

Then I guess I don't have much to worry about with the cats, I said.

Don't listen to him, MacLeod said. What does he know, the locals are imbeciles, that's the first thing you should learn. The cats are probably watching us right now, getting ready to attack. Let's get to the hut already, he said.

It DIDN'T take me long before I loved the hut we called home but that MacLeod always referred to as the hut. I would take my shoes off before climbing the steps made of cleaved bamboo shafts and I would walk across the cool straw mats whose faint smell of straw was warm and rich and I would breathe in deeply, smelling also the spicy sambal and nasi goreng that Tekul's wife, Kidul, would be cooking in the kitchen.

Norman was with Kidul. He was playing with a leather way-ang puppet on the floor one day while Kidul fried rice for the nasi goreng and said to Norman, I will now tell you the story of the ogre who made the volcano. I stood in the doorway of the kitchen, watching my son and listening to Kidul's story too.

The ogre lived in the central plateau, which was ruled by a king who had a beautiful daughter. When the ogre set eyes on the daughter, he fell deeply in love. The king did not want his daughter to marry the horrible creature. But what could he do? If he said no to the terrible ogre, the ogre might destroy his kingdom. The king decided to challenge the ogre to see how strong he was and to see if he was worthy of his daughter. I challenge you to carve a deep valley by dawn with only half a coconut shell, the king told the ogre. The king imagined the task would be too hard for the ogre to complete, but the ogre was a fast worker, and as the night progressed it looked as though the ogre would complete the task. What can I do? said the king to himself.

The king became very worried. I will not have my daughter marry that terrible ogre! He called together his servants at midnight. Pound the rice now! he ordered, which is what the servants always did each morning at sunrise. The king knew that the sound of the servants pounding the rice would excite the roosters and make them crow, because they knew that when the sound of the rice being pounded began, then the sun would soon rise.

The ogre, busy at work with his half a coconut shell, heard the roosters crowing. It must be dawn. I have failed! I will never marry the king's beautiful daughter now! he cried in anger and then stormed off, throwing down his coconut shell on the ground, whose shape became a volcano, and then he jumped into the flames blazing from its crater.

Look out the window, Kidul said, and what you see is his coconut shell turned upside down. That is our volcano, she said. And the foul smell at the top of the volcano comes from the ogre's body that continues to burn in the crater.

BETWEEN LINES

No REPLY CAME from the Dutch consulate or from her daughter. But she was used to her daughter not responding. She knew MacLeod had never shown her daughter the letters she sent. Here in prison, though, she was left to believe that her letters were never mailed, that they were sitting opened on Bouchardon's desk. He now knew the tale of the ogre too, because that is what she wrote to her daughter about, asking her if she remembered the tale, and she told it to her again in case she didn't only because she liked the tale and she liked thinking about her daughter and Norman before Norman died, and she wanted her daughter to remember her brother the way she remembered him, playing with a wayang kulit puppet and casting shadows on the wall with it while he told Kidul's stories from the island or stories he would make up himself. Bouchardon most likely held the letters up to the lamp, looking between the lines for signs of secret ink she might have used. Perhaps there was something in tears that could act like invisible ink, because all that ended up between the lines on the pages to her daughter were tears she did not catch in time after they fell from her eyes and onto a page about an ogre, a king, and a beautiful daughter.

NOT A NEW BEGINNING

MacLeod was hardly home and when he was home he was busy searching the house. He was out on the balcony, moving aside great potted plants of bougainvillea and lotus and rubber trees whose paddle-shaped leaves draped heavily over his balding head as he knelt and slid the pot aside, searching for hidden scorpions or a poisonous naga curled at the ceramic base.

After he had decided the house was safe, he would play with Norman. He liked showing Norman how to march and how to hold a gun. You can be just like Papa, he told Norman. But once Norman pulled, from the back of his pants, a kris dagger Tekul had carved for him out of the root of a mangrove. This is much better than a gun, Norman told MacLeod. My kris dagger is magic and can kill thieves without me. It can even stop giant waves from forming in the sea and it can stop lava flowing from volcanoes! MacLeod took the carved dagger from Norm's hands and broke it on the balcony's wooden railing. He then threw the pieces off into the garden, where they fell on jasmine flowers, snapping off their blossoms. Their scent drifted up to where we stood on the balcony and where MacLeod was now telling me it was all my fault and that I never should have let the servants tell the boy such stories. Poor Norman cried at the sight of his broken kris dagger and so I tried to glue it back together for him, but the glue would not hold and I cursed it and held Norman in my arms and told him I could do what the kris dagger could do. I would kill thieves for him, I would stop giant waves for him, and I would stop lava from flowing, and Norman asked me how I could do all that and I told him that when you love someone as much as I loved him, these things were possible, and he laughed and said I could not do all that and I said that I felt that I could. From the other room, MacLeod called out, Don't listen to your mother's stories, son, she can't do all those things.

One day I walked into the shops in town that sold dresses made in the Netherlands. They hung in solid dark colors on their hangers and I looked through all of them, but what caught my eye wasn't hanging in a shop. It was what I saw on the island women walking down the street. Their bright silk sarongs, covered in designs of flowers whose petals seemed to burst from the cloth, were more beautiful than any dresses I had ever seen. Wearing a sarong got looks from other officers' wives, who told me they could not imagine wearing something so garish and loud. I wore the sarongs every day and the silk cloth whispered as I walked and a quiet breeze stirred and reached up, awakening something between my legs.

When I walked down the path, the silver leaf monkeys shrieked loudly and swung from vine to vine, following me as I went. Kidul showed me how she could tear the skin off a mango with her teeth and took me to a cave where bats hung upside down and covered the rock wall and ceiling so that the cave seemed to be made of bats and not of stone at all. When rats crossed our path, Kidul pointed out that they were not as fat and their tails not as long as the twenty-five rats Tekul had caught and given to Kidul's father on the day of their marriage.

Rats were your dowry? I said, and when I told Kidul that there had been no dowry for my father at my marriage, Kidul lowered her eyes and shook her head and then she suddenly lifted up her head and her dark eyes shone, and she said, Tekul is still a good rat catcher and I know he can catch at least twenty-five again and he could give them to your father! And then I made Kidul laugh, telling her how the officers' wives would shriek like the silver leaf monkeys if they had to sail back home with twenty-five fat, long-tailed island rats. Then Kidul showed me how to braid my hair and weave in the pink and white blossoms that lay on the forest floor.

MacLeod sometimes came to me late at night after he had been at the officers' club or with island women he bought by the hour. I sat up in bed, ready when he came, but I think he would have liked it better if I were asleep or if I were angry at him or if I at least told him no or tried to push him off. I tried to enjoy myself, I tried to please MacLeod. Fat, old Heer Wybrandus from the school in the Netherlands had been a good teacher. I knew what to do, but afterward MacLeod would say that I was no more than a whore. Sometimes he would take my sarong and rip it in half and then in quarters and throw it at me while I lay in bed after our exertions, not being able to tell if it was my sweat drying on my skin or his. Then he would go into the living room and sleep on the bamboo couch, which was too short for him, and in the early morning hours I could hear the creak of bamboo as he pushed his feet against the couch's arm, trying to make himself fit. Then, in the heat of the darkness with a lotus as large as the moon growing out my window, I thought of my walk across the cold sand sea to Ameland, and I knew that Java was not the new beginning for MacLeod and me that I had dreamed it could be.

CROSSING THROUGH PUDDLES

THE MORE MACLEOD DRANK, the more she learned what there was to learn from the island and the more she wore her sarongs, drank jasmine tea, and ate nasi goreng with her fingertips, the more MacLeod was found on the sides of dusty roads with his uniform dirty and his hat on the ground beside him and butterflies landing and spreading flat their wings and sunning themselves on his bald head beaded with sweat and smelling of bourbon.

Not unlike, she thought, her visits with Bouchardon. The more he didn't talk, the more she did. The more he tapped his pencil on his pad of paper, the more she rattled off names of Germans she knew, the more he bit his nails and chewed them between his front teeth, then swallowed them, the more she told him about the lovers she had had. She told him the color of their hair and the cologne they used and the gifts they had given her, rings they bought off other women in restaurants if in passing she mentioned she liked them. She knew the make of her lovers' overcoats, which they took off their own backs and threw over puddles so she could cross streets without wetting her shoes. She knew Bouchardon would think these were all clues to prove her guilt and she fed them to him, wondering when he would realize that what she was telling him were just the memories of a middle-aged woman who once had many lovers, and they were not the memories of some coldhearted spy intent on the defeat of the Allied forces.

THE RAINS

I BECAME PREGNANT with Non when the lyang-lyang grass was at its highest, and what that meant, Kidul told me, was that the rains were about to begin. The rains were like the sound of ocean waves never ceasing, or the buzz of insects never ceasing, only worse because it was rain and walking in it you did not wear thongs that could splash the water back to you high up your leg and you went barefoot instead, wading ankle-deep through float-ing battered palm leaves over small rocks and pebbles that skated beneath you under the soles of your feet as you went from here to there, your sarong pasted to your legs, outlining the muscles in your thighs and the bone in your kneecap and the sarong's colors running, so at night, before bed, when you took it off, you were mottled green or blue or red from the dye and looked as though you had come from the forest, and were in the process of changing, of shedding skin or growing fur, working yourself into a primitive state so that you were the ideal camouflage creature and could sit on the forest floor and never be seen.

WHEN MACLEOD found out, he said, It's a boy, it better be a boy.

Who knows, I said, and I shrugged my shoulders, and he asked me what that was, was it some kind of gesture Kidul had taught me? Was it to conjure the gods or keep back evil spirits or raise the dead or keep the dead dead?

I said, I'd like to go to the officers' party tonight.

What I liked about the other officers was that each one danced differently. One danced as if he were constantly afraid I was going to fall and he held me tight. Another danced as if I were something sticky he could not shake off the ends of his fingers. Still another danced as if there were something as large as a column between us. One even danced as if the floor were on fire and one danced as if he were grinding out a cigar and one danced as if he had lost a gold coin and was searching for it. Another danced as if his knees hurt, and later I learned that they did. One danced as if he wanted to make love to me, and later I learned that he did. One danced as if he had made love to me before and I had to tell him he never had and he said I just didn't remember. One danced like a boy, and he was my Norman. I held him up in my arms and twirled around the room and kissed the backs of his baby-fat hands as he waved to his papa, who sat at the table with his chin on his chest sound asleep.

At first I spent hours watching the rain come down. Kidul or Norman or MacLeod would have to pull me away from the balcony. I could not believe that Java did not just float away. I started to believe that indeed we were floating away. How would we not know it? What was there to anchor us to always one spot in the sea? I wanted to feel the dry earth, but there was none to feel. Even the soil in the houseplants was black and spongy, as wet as if it had been raining as hard inside the house as it was outside.

Once there was a different sound to the rain. It came like a knock at the door and I cocked my head to listen, thinking maybe it was changing its gears, getting ready to stop, but it was what it sounded like, a soft rap at the bamboo door of my home.

It was the officer who danced as though he wanted to make love to me. The rain dripped off his hat and the rain dripped off the ends of his fingers and I watched it slide in the changing shapes of continents and landmasses off the tops of his polished black shoes onto my straw mat. He was there to let me know I could think of him as a trade.

A trade for what? I said.

A Javanese girl I saw your husband with last night, he said.

THE FAIR TRADE

HE SAT on my couch, his long legs partly open as he used the towel I had handed him to wipe his hair of the rain. His eyes were different shades of green and I spent time just looking at their colors, not trying to read what he was telling me with them. There was even yellow in his eyes. He reached across and put his hand on my leg and his thumb seemed to lead the way, traveling up toward the inside of my thigh where he said he could feel a pulse. That's where he put his lips first after he opened up wide the slit in my sarong. His lips still felt wet from the rain.

I'm not interested, I said. My son is sleeping in his room and his nurse is with him and she sleeps lightly, I said, she's afraid of monkey spirits taking her up in their hands and their feet and carrying her away.

I showed him to the door while he told me his name was Willem and that he would be back, because he knew that there would be plenty more Javanese girls and that I had a ways to go before settling the score with my husband.

In the dark, in my bed alone, with the sound of the falling rain, I remembered how his lips felt on my leg and I remembered how the weight of him felt, the warm crown of his head nudging toward my pubis.

*   *   *

TEKUL SOMETIMES held an umbrella over my head as I walked, while he walked with the water cascading down his face. I told him to join me under the umbrella, but he shook his head, Master MacLeod would not like that. When we arrived at a shop, Tekul would wait outside for me, holding the umbrella closed and by his side. When I left the shop, he instantly popped the umbrella open again so that I would not feel a drop of rain. Once I told him no to the umbrella and we walked back toward the house with it closed and up under Tekul's arm. Let's pretend it's not raining, I told him. The rain came down in bullets. It had a force that seemed to be able to bend the tops of Tekul's ears downward. It loosened my bun and my black hair spun out from my head and any curl that my hair had was made flat and my hair stretched down long, covering my breasts.

On the street, Tekul saw his mother, who was having trouble holding the imported cheese and tea she had bought in town for the officer she worked for and I told Tekul to run and walk her back using the umbrella so her employer's supplies would not get ruined and so she would not be blamed for being careless. I walked back alone toward the house and when I turned a corner on the road, I almost ran into Willem. At that moment, the rain rained even harder and I could not hear what he was saying to me. He grabbed me by the elbow and he steered me past a few houses until he came to a house where he produced a key from his pocket and opened up the door.

Welcome, he said. This time it was he who went to fetch a towel. He did not hand the towel to me, though. He stood behind me and dried my hair for me and then he turned me toward him and he held the towel over my blouse on my breasts and he moved his hand in circles this way, lifting and pressing against me, his fingers moving through the towel, his thumb finding my nipple and circling it over and over again.

He moved the towel over my buttocks and then in front of me, up and down my thighs, and this time he did not split my sarong wide. Instead, with his teeth, he pulled the knot free and it fell to the floor and both his hands now worked at drying me and went down to my ankles and he dried them tenderly and after that is when he let the towel go and he started his kisses there, on the bones of my ankles.

I'm with child, I told him.

Good, then you can't get pregnant again, he said, and he picked me up in his arms and carried me to his bed. I turned him over so that I was on top of him and his green eyes flecked with yellow smiled and I was thankful to see their color after having had so many days of gray skies and bleak rain. I unbuttoned his uniform and his shirt so that they lay splayed open next to him on the bed like the wings of a bat flat against the wall of a cave.

When I let him enter me, the size of him took my breath away and he wanted to know if I was all right and I told him he would take some getting used to and he said he liked that I used those words because he wanted me to get used to him.

Afterward I noticed that my damp hair and his wet uniform and our sex had made his sheets all wet and I began to remove them for him but he stopped and asked what I was doing and then I realized Tekul might be looking for me. Leaving, I said, and I ran out the door and he ran after me, stopping in the doorway with his uniform and shirt still unbuttoned, calling my name, calling, Margaretha, Margaretha. Later, when I was far from his house, I could still hear him calling me and I knew that I was just imagining I heard my name and that what I was really hearing was only the rain.

From then on, that is what the rain kept saying. All through the night, it was calling my name and I tried to stop it. I tried to sleep with pillows over my head. I took a blanket to go and sleep next to MacLeod on the floor because I knew his snoring was so loud it might drown out the sound of my name in the rain, but MacLeod wasn't on the couch and he was still out, widening his lead, scoring more points by sleeping with more women.

I went to check on Norman and he was dreaming. I could see his eyes moving back and forth beneath his eyelids. He was breathing so quietly it seemed as if he were hardly breathing at all and I shook him, wanting to wake him, thinking maybe I could read to him or we could play patty-cake and my name in the rain could not be heard above our clapping. But Norman did not wake, his eyes stopped moving back and forth and so he stopped dreaming, then he turned away from me, mumbling something I could not hear, and, Damn, I thought, why are children's mouths so small?

SO MANY QUESTIONS

She told the doctor as he listened to her heart that his stethoscope looked old, as if the rats had started gnawing at it, that maybe he had been too long here in the prison. He said it wasn't as if he were a prisoner, that he could of course leave whenever he wanted to. He had a garden at home that he worked on. He grew beans and lettuces and radishes. He said he would bring her some next time, but of course he couldn't and it was just something to say, the way people say bless you after you've sneezed and they say it without even thinking.

She told him she had spit up blood that morning when she coughed, she showed him how when she tried to hold her hand out steadily it trembled, she ran a comb through her hair and showed him all the strands that came away with each downward stroke of her arm, she said that when she was tired she knew red lines in her eyes would appear, looking like a meandering section of forked and branching roads drawn on a map in the middle of nowhere. She asked if she had those red lines now in her eyes, and then she said, Of course you can't see, how could you see in this poor light? but she knew the red lines were there, she could almost feel them there under her lids, as if the lines were raised

49

and her eyes were some sort of a raised map where one could trace with his fingertips the roads to nowhere.

He gave her pills for sleeping and her dreams were as deep as her sleep, and when she woke she felt as if she were fighting through layers and layers of the dreams to break through the surface.

She never knew when Bouchardon would call for her. When he did they sent a guard to escort her to his office. The guard waited a moment while she changed into her street shoes and the dark blue dress she had worn the first day she was taken to prison. She asked for a glass of water and the guard gave it to her and she used it to look at her reflection and then she placed two fingers in the glass and used the water to smooth back the coarse graying hairs at her temples, which had come undone from the bun at the back of her head.

She was still feeling the sleeping pills when she sat down in the chair Bouchardon offered her and she hoped her answers to his questions would not come slowly or sound dim-witted.

He had so many questions. How much money did the Germans give you? Where was the bedroom your maid slept in?

Did your maid wear a sleep mask? Did your maid take sleeping pills? Did your maid stay up and read in bed at night?

Are you asking if my maid was a spy? she said. He bit his fingernails and chewed them, answering between clenched teeth so that he could still keep hold of the nail he was working on chewing without having it fall onto the floor of his office.

Was she? he said.

No, of course not, she said.

Do you know for sure? he said.

She was my maid, she said. She brought my feather boas to

the cleaners, she boiled the water for my tea, she lined up the shoes in my closet.

She accepted money for you from your lovers, did she not? he asked.

At times, because then she would send it on to me wherever I was.

Where was that? he asked.

What do you mean? she said.

Where were you when she sent it on to you? he said.

Anywhere, everywhere, she said. I performed in Italy, Berlin, Spain, France, The Hague, you know that, she said.

He nodded his head. He tapped his pencil on his pad. Then he went to the window and tapped his fingers on the pane.

I'm not a German spy, she said. His fingers kept tapping. Then he turned around.

That's all for today, he said.

MATA HARI

My name had to change, I was tired of the sound of it being drummed out in the rain. Kidul was the one who suggested Mata Hari. She said it meant the eye of dawn, the sunrise. I liked the name, I did not hear it in the rain. I imagined it was the sound rays of sunlight made as they shone down on the forest floor and dried the soaked earth.

MacLeod laughed when he first heard Kidul call me Mata Hari. More like eye of the storm, he said, and he slapped his knee and laughed some more.

Norman climbed into his lap and MacLeod checked his hair, looking closely at his scalp and saying that other officers said their children were getting lice from the servants. Check them, MacLeod told me.

Our servants don't have lice. If they did they would have let me know, I told him.

You trust them too much, MacLeod said.

When he said that I realized that the only one I didn't trust was MacLeod. He took Norman off his knee and then he left and did not come back that night.

Norman called me Mama Hari and I loved it when he said it and picked him up and hugged him and he hugged me back and whispered in my ear, I didn't tell on you, I didn't tell Papa I heard you speak Malay.

Saya tidak mengerti, I don't understand, I said to Kidul when Kidul asked if I had money for a badak's horn.

You place it under your bed when the baby comes, Kidul answered.

Then I said again, Saya tidak mengerti, what do I need a badak's horn for?

You'll have no pain if you do, Kidul said. The badak horn is powerful. If you don't have enough money to buy one, you can rent one. Tekul knows someone who will rent you one for a good price.

Berapa? I said.

Maybe seribu, Kidul said.

I said that for that kind of money I'd rather have the birthing pains and keep the money to buy new cloth for sarongs.

GIBBONS CAME in through the door that night. They went to my dresser and took my hair combs and they went into the kitchen and took forks and they went into Norman's room and took a toy metal car and Kidul and I woke up when they came in and we yelled at them to go away and the gibbons shrieked and knocked over a table and a chair and one pissed on the wall and another struck my mirror with the back of its hairy hand when it saw its own reflection. When MacLeod found out he was sure the gibbons would take Norman the next time they came so he sat in a chair on the balcony at night and with his hand on his pistol he waited for the gibbons to come back. He almost shot Willem when Willem came in the middle of the night. The bullet missed, though, and bore into the ground instead.

I thought you were a gibbon, MacLeod said, apologizing from the balcony after hearing Willem cry out and then MacLeod looked at his watch and turned and looked at me leaning over the balcony in nothing but a silk robe to see what was going on and then he realized why Willem had come in the middle of the night and he put the pistol to my temple and said, You are disgusting.

I turned and went back to bed and MacLeod threw the covers off me and pulled me up by the wrists and threw me out the front door and down the bamboo steps. I caught up to Willem in the rain. He took off his jacket and held it over my head and together we entered his house.

Will he come and shoot me? Willem asked.

No, I don't think so, I said, and Willem said he didn't think so either. I told him that by now MacLeod was drunk and asleep in Norman's room. Sometimes when he was very drunk he would go in there by Norman's bed and on his knees he would stare at his son and fall asleep with his head on his son's bed, holding his son's hand. In the morning when I kissed Norman, his hair would smell of his father's liquored breath and I would tell Kidul to give Norman a bath with rosewater and later I would feed him fresh buah and let him drink sips of my morning kopi to help take away the smell.

I lay back in Willem's bed and he undid the belt of my silk robe. I thought he would cast it aside, but then he used the belt between my legs, sliding it over and over again, and then lightly kissing me through it while it rested on my pubis. Then he held the belt by both ends and slid it back and forth through me so that there was more pressure and his kisses were now deeper and his tongue was there, probing into me through the cloth where my wetness met the wetness of his mouth, and then finally when he unbuttoned his pants and he entered me, the belt entered along with him, and he drove into me, pushing deeper and deeper with each thrust, and just as I climaxed he withdrew the belt from inside me and I screamed because I had never felt anything like it before.

I left his place before the black of the rainy night turned into the gray of a rainy day. Before I left he told me to wait and he reached inside his pocket and he gave me a roll of guilders. He did not say anything to me as he gave them to me, and I did not say anything to him. Maybe I nodded, but that was all.

I showed Kidul and she said that was more than enough to rent a badak's horn and I told her, Good, go rent one, because maybe when the time came I would need it after all.

MacLeod liked to tell me about the other women he saw Willem with. He likes big breasts, all of his whores are like cows past milking, he said. You must be a disappointment in comparison, he said.

NON

THE BADAK, or one-horned rhino, was shy. I never saw one. I went to the river to look, but all I saw were macaques crashing and screeching through the branches, and beneath them, in the muddy water, a crocodile cruised while onshore a thick python lay curled, snug in the hollow of a banyan tree.

With some leftover guilders from Willem I thought of asking Tekul to buy me a curving kris dagger because I thought it would give me strength. The goddess of the southern seas was married eight times, but each time her husband died on the wedding night. For her ninth husband she chose a holy man, who in the wali tradition stayed up praying rather than make love to his new wife. In the middle of the cold, dark night, his praying was interrupted by an eerie sound and he saw a poisonous snake on the pillow by the head of his bride. He grabbed the snake and threw it to the floor, where, in an instant, it turned into a shining kris dagger.

You can marry a kris dagger, Kidul told me.

I'm already married, I said.

Yes, I know, Kidul said, but still you can marry one if you'd like. The holy men in my village will perform the rites.

I went to her village and a gamelan orchestra played their strange instruments while shadow dramas were played against a skin made from a banteng hide, which hung from the branches of an ironwood tree. The shadow drama was played for hours and Kidul and her mother wove in between those of us who sat on the ground and watched and they offered us sweet nasi goreng from baskets they held on their heads.

It was the old story of Prince Rama who was born to rid the world of the demon Ravana. Rama's wife, Sita, was captured by Ravana, and to get her back Rama created an army of monkeys led by the monkey king and the monkey general. They pounced down on Ravana and slew him, and Sita was returned to her prince. It was not only the story I left the village remembering, but the sounds of the gamelan orchestra whose steady drumbeat followed me out of the forest like a lover who would not let me go, and I felt it pull at my wrists as tight as a gibbon's grip and I almost stayed and dreamed of living in Kidul's village, where I would rise every day just to sit on the ground and listen to the music of the wayang kulit shadow drama and at night I would sleep on a reed mat and dream of the river.

You did not stay for the marriage to the kris dagger, Kidul said as she walked next to me, and I said I never wanted to marry again, once in my life was more than enough, and anyway, I said, I had found a new lover back there more powerful than the kris dagger and it was the music from the gamelan orchestra.

Really? Kidul asked, and I turned and looked at Kidul and touched her brown cheek with the palm of my hand and said, It is just a way of speaking.

THE PRICE OF CLOTH

MACLEOD WROTE LETTERS to his sister in the Netherlands, telling her how his wife was like a child and as the months went by she seemed to grow even younger. He was afraid for his son and his unborn child and thought one day some harm would come to his son because of his wife forgetting to feed him or clothe him because she was too stupid and busy flirting with other officers, fitting herself into sarongs and learning Malay when he had forbidden her to speak it. He wrote that he would divorce his wife if it weren't for the children and he wanted them to have a mother, if only it weren't her.

> Dear Brother, I am sending you the tailored shirts you requested. The tailor said he hoped your measurements have not changed since last time because those are the measurements he used as a guide. Also, the price of the cloth has risen by two guilders, and his workmanship by one.
>
> As for Margaretha, I am sorry to hear what a drain she must be on you. You must be strong. If she behaves like a child, then you are right to treat her like one and discipline her. She was lucky to have found such a wonderful husband as you, and it saddens me to hear how unappreciated you

are. Let's hope there will come a time in her life when she will be ashamed of the way she treats you and that she will make a change for the better, at least for the sake of the children. For now, try and do your best to weather it out. If all else fails, then I'm sure that it would not take you long to find a more suitable wife if you were to come back home. Oh, and how I wish you would come back! I'd very much like to see baby Norman again. Although he must be quite the little man by now and not the plump bundle he was the last time I saw him. Plant a kiss on his cheek for me.

Your sister,

Louise

THE BADAK'S HORN

I THOUGHT the badak's horn beneath my bed did help. When the time came, Kidul placed it on a china plate and on the plate she lay a square of batik cloth so that the horn's pointed end faced upward. When I saw how Kidul placed the horn, I laughed and knew why the badak horn helped relieve birthing pains. The woman in labor was so worried the whole time, thinking that if the bed broke and the loosely filled horsehair mattress fell down, then she'd be impaled right up through the back. So the pain of the labor was lessened by fear of death by the horn of a badak.

Just when I thought I could not take the pain much longer, I thought of my walk across the sea to Ameland. I was there again, the dark sand beneath my feet and the cool ocean mist blowing across like white dust in the breeze.

Kidul cleaned and washed the baby I named Non and wrapped her in a cloth and took her out of the room to show MacLeod his new daughter. I watched through the open door and before MacLeod sat up from the couch to see the baby, he asked, Boy or girl? And when Kidul said, Girl, MacLeod stood but did not walk toward Kidul to see the girl. Instead he walked out of the house to go for a drink at the officers' club. I imagined the other men asking, Can you handle two women in the house, MacLeod?

while buying him drinks. And MacLeod shaking his head, saying, I can't even handle the one.

But MacLeod was back that night, and again he helped take care of his new baby and he worried about the small animal sounds Non made in her sleep and when she woke crying with hunger he was the one who picked her up and made sure she was nursing properly from my breast and while I nursed he placed his hand on Non's sheet in her crib so that her bed would be warm when she was put back down. When I fastened the diaper, MacLeod said, Let me do it, you're pricking the poor thing, and I left and went to sit on the balcony and listen to the thrum of the insects in the forest, thinking that this too was the beginning of my daughter being taken away from me.

OVER THE WALL

IN THE PRISON YARD she noticed a hair again clinging to the same rock it had the day before, and the day before that. Each time she took the hair and let it sail away, over the wall of the prison. It was a blond hair, and when the sun was bright she could not follow the hair and she could not see if it was sailing away up over the prison wall, or if it was merely falling to the ground.

Sister Leonide said she had a visitor. Clunet was her lawyer, he also at one time had been her lover, but he was now so old that his eyes were always wet and seemed to float in his head and it was difficult to tell if he was looking at her or at something to the left or right of her. He had no news from the Dutch consulate. He was not allowed to write many letters either, he explained to her, because it was a military trial, an espionage case to make matters worse. He was not allowed to come with her to see Bouchardon, and neither did he have the power to speak with any witnesses who may be able to help her.

No one knows you are in prison, he said.

No one? said Sister Leonide.

Mata Hari was relieved. She did not want Non to know what had happened to her.

The next day another blond hair was clinging to the same

stone in the prison yard. She took it off and again let it fly in the breeze. She became convinced that another prisoner was putting her hairs there so she could, bit by bit, set herself free. In days to follow, Mata Hari imagined that after all the hairs of the woman were set free, then what would follow would be bits of the woman's skin, her nails, shavings even of her bone, which Mata Hari herself would dutifully pick from the stone and send up over the prison wall.

NOTHING TO DO WITH MATA HARI

WITH MACLEOD STROKING Non's head and smiling while she nursed from me, I thought for a moment that his smile was for both of us, but it wasn't. When he looked at me, his smile disappeared. I wondered if my hair looked untidy, if my dressing gown was soiled with my leaking milk or even if it smelled faintly sour from milk that had stained it earlier in the day. He left the room and I could hear him in the kitchen telling Kidul that the satay she cooked was too hot, and that the spices made the baby's belly ache. From now on, he told Kidul, Margaretha is to eat plain white rice.

I ate the white rice in front of him, and when he was not there I feasted on the nasi goreng or the tender babi satay or cap cai with spicy sauce as if I had craved them and had not eaten them for years, when it had been only yesterday.

Your boyfriend's been sent back home, MacLeod said to me one day. Who will fuck you now?

———

WHEN NON started to teethe, MacLeod curled his finger and gave it to her to chew on, sweetened with some gula or susu. When it was time for bed, he took his finger and stroked the bridge of her nose so that her eyes would keep closing, until they finally stayed closed and she slept.

He cut Norman's hair in the garden and the hair fell in half-moon shapes next to jasmine leaves and later MacLeod picked up one of the half-moons and put it in an envelope. *Norm's hair, 3 years old,* he wrote on the envelope and he kept it in his top dresser drawer.

MacLeod answered his own question for me. At night he came to me and he tore off my stained dressing gown and he buried his head in my swollen breasts, where my milk spurted onto his hair, and he forced himself into me, while with one hand I reached across the bed in the dark, searching for a towel to press upon my breasts and stop the flow.

If I hated him it was never at these times. At these times I could forgive him because I knew it was the liquor making him rough. I could forgive him because the act seemed as if it had nothing to do with me.

I felt more hatred for him when he told me that I was, for example, clipping Norman's or Non's nails the wrong way. He said I should use two angled cuts on each little nail, instead of one cut across the nail, which bent the nail, he said, and it was painful to the children. And I felt terrible thinking I had hurt them in any way at all and so I kissed each one of their small fingertips and told them how sorry I was and that I loved them and I would never hurt them again.

I felt more hatred for MacLeod when he came home and I was sitting with Norman in my lap, putting on a show for him with his leather wayang kulit puppet, and Norman broke away from our game and ran to him, yelling, Papa, Papa! I felt hatred for him when Non fell and scraped her knee and I went to pick her up, and Non cried even more when I picked her up and held out both her arms in the direction of her father, so that he would be the one to kiss her knee and hold her tight instead.

What was easier than hating MacLeod was leaving it up to him to cut their nails. But I missed having them sit on me when I cut their nails and I missed holding their small hands in mine, my face close to them, breathing in the sweetness of their soft skin and hair, storing up the scent of them inside me, trying to fill up my lungs and body with it as much as possible so that their smells became a part of me and could last me a lifetime.

What was easier than hating him was not to run and pick up Non when she fell, but to let MacLeod do it. I would leave the hut and take a walk instead. When I returned, he would be with the children in the garden, they would be fighting a battle with toy guns, and Norman would be wearing his father's hat, and Non would be yelling, Bam, bam, as she fired off imaginary artillery, and no one would notice I was home after I'd walked silently up the bamboo steps and across the straw mat in my bare feet, dusty and brown from walking on the ground.

And when night came I lay awake thinking and wondering what I would do if something were to take my Norm and my Non away from me. I wondered what I could do to keep them with me and so, before sleep, I imagined our hut had doors made of thick steel. Nothing could enter through them, not fire or flood or thieves or sickness, and I shut those doors in succession from all directions, north, south, west, east, and it was not until

I had pictured these doors all shut and locked that I was able to fall asleep. But at times I wondered if someone already living inside the house was more dangerous than anything else that could possibly enter it.

SISTER LEONIDE

Sister Leonide said she had become a nun late in life. For years she had cleaned hotel rooms and she said you learn a lot about people by cleaning up after them. You learn how they wake up in the morning, if they jump out of bed or if they slide out of it or if, when they do get up, they sit on the edge of the bed first before gathering some kind of strength to stand all the way up. If they left both slippers next to the bed after they put on their clothes, or if one slipper was in the bathroom and the other by the dresser, then she felt she knew who they were, without ever having met them or talked to them. If the mirror needed cleaning in their room, because there were fingerprint marks on it from them leaning against it, looking closely at themselves, then she felt she knew what kind of person was renting the room.

When she walked into some rooms she could feel the pain of the person's mind as if the person were still in the room. She would immediately notice a drawer shut too tight, slammed so that it recessed more than the other drawers, and when she pulled the drawer out so that it was flush with the others she could see the dovetail joinery of the drawer looking looser than before, jarred as it was. She would notice multiple rings on the

table where a glass had been picked up and been set down again
so many times that she knew the drinker must have been frantic
with worry or overcome by anger. She noticed where the pile
of the carpet had been pressed down in a spot by the window,
where the person's feet had stood for hours at a time, looking
outside, waiting for someone to come or to leave or for something to happen.

It was cleaning rooms that made her realize she wanted to
help people. She knew the only way she could help people was
if she had something to give them. She didn't have anything, at
the time. So she went and married God. After she had God, she
knew she now had something to give. It was very easy, she said.
Cleaning rooms was harder, she said.

Mata Hari asked Sister Leonide what she noticed about her
cell. Did it cry out that she was a traitorous spy?

I can tell by the way your pillow is pressed down all over when
you wake in the morning that you have had head-tossing dreams,
because in your sleep you thought turning over would make the
bad dreams end, and let a good dream in, Sister Leonide said.

Mata Hari knelt down in front of her. Sister Leonide's silver
cross was cold at her cheek. She looked into the blackness of her
habit.

I have walked across the sea, she whispered.

I know you are brave, she said, because you do not finish the
food on your plate and you think you will go on living and that
you do not need the food, because you think you will be freed
someday and there will be better food to eat. Then she stroked
her head. You should finish your food, she whispered.

I have walked across the sea, Mata Hari told her, and she did
not finish her food. The velvet horn tangled in my feet, wet blad-

A SHOT AT NOTHING

KIDUL SAID Non looked like me. Same hair, same eyes, Kidul said.

Nonsense, said MacLeod, she's a MacLeod through and through, he said. She already runs this house better than you, MacLeod said.

Perhaps it was true. Non never had to be told to put away her toys after she was done with them, I sometimes thought she enjoyed putting things away more than she enjoyed playing with them. What seemed to please her was seeing her toys up on a shelf, where she could not even reach them.

Norman, on the other hand, couldn't stand to have his toys put away. When he stopped playing castle wars with his blocks and wandered off to play robber demon with his puppets I would tell him that if he was finished he should put his blocks away, but then he would say, I'm not finished with them! And he would run back to his blocks and start playing with them again and I would tell him to then put away his puppets and he would run back to his puppets and say, I'm not finished with them! And the afternoon would go this way, where he rotated from one group of toys to the next, caught in a balancing act of make-believe.

After watching Norman at play, Tekul said to me, The boy is

more like you, and I nodded. MacLeod, though, turned to Tekul. Shut up, he said, don't you have some work to do?! Tekul left, holding a mallet. The bamboo steps were becoming loose, and he had to hammer them gently back into place. The tapping of his mallet started off the gibbons in the trees and their shrieks made MacLeod grab his gun, and he stood on the balcony, shooting again at what he could not see.

A LOT, OR NOTHING

IF YOU WANT to be a spy for the French, you can go to 282 boulevard Saint-Germain in Paris, but you must go first to tell the captain, a bearded man named Ladoux, that you are there because you need a pass to get into a war zone known as Vittel. You are going there because you want to take the waters, because your health is poor. Pat lightly at your chest, as you tell him this. When he says he knows you want to go to Vittel to visit your Russian lover, tell him, Yes, but the waters would also be a good idea. He will then tell you that the British know about you, that they think you are a German spy. Shake your head when he says this, tell him you thought something like that was going on, that you had noticed the British trailing you in and out of your hotel, that they peered in at you while you were seated in a coffee shop, that they had gone through your coat pockets while you were out of your room, that you noticed your coats hanging in the closet, the pockets turned inside out, looking like the ears of rabbits, and your closet some warren. He will shake his head. His black hair won't sway as he does, though, as it is smeared with too much brilliantine, and he will say that he did not think you were a German spy and he will say that the British are as nervous as rabbits. He will then ask if you love France. Tell him the truth, tell him you love France. Tell him you are a Francophile. He will ask if you are prepared to help the French war effort with great services. Act surprised, because you are. You hadn't thought that simply going to him for a pass to see your Russian lover in a war zone would turn you into a spy.

Would you do it? he asks.

I've never thought about it, you say.

You must be very expensive, he says.

That's for sure, you say.

What do you think such work is worth? he says.

A lot, or nothing, you say.

THE GODDESS
OF THE SOUTHERN SEAS

I SAW WILLEM again. Not in his hut, but in the thick bamboo forest. His green eyes glittered inside the head of a leopard. I remembered I was supposed to run, but I didn't. I just looked into his eyes, amazed that they were the same as Willem's. I thought for a moment that it was possible that MacLeod had changed Willem into a leopard and I even called out his name in the night, but there was no answer from the green-eyed leopard, only the sound of a ghost bird's wings flapping above. For a second I looked up at the ghost bird, blocking out the light of the moon, and when I looked down, the leopard was gone.

I was angry at MacLeod when I returned home. I felt that he was responsible for sending Willem away, across the sea. He wasn't even at home for me to get angry at, though, and so I walked to town. I knew where the brothel was.

He was in room 14. When I opened the door he was on top of a Javanese girl whose long braid hung off the edge of the bed, its brushlike end painting the floor, back and forth, as he moved inside of her. She turned and looked at me and all I could see of her was one of her eyes. It was a strange eye, clouded like an old faithful dog's eyes. Its cloudiness seemed almost white, as if light were trying to come through from the other side. I had planned on stopping him and yelling at him and cursing at him, and who knows what else, throwing things at him, but I didn't do any of it. I didn't feel like having everyone in town knowing what was going on between us. Instead I closed the door, and as I did I realized that the room number, number 14, was probably the same as the girl's age.

I MADE SURE they weren't wearing green. Norman's suit for swimming was black, and Non's was black and white stripes. We were at Pelabuhan Ratu, where the goddess of the southern seas was said to live in its waters. Grief-stricken, she once threw herself over the cliff and into the deep. She is said to live there still, calling lovers to the shore, enticing them with a sweet smell of lotus on warm nights and making them join her in her watery world. If anyone drowned in the strong current, it was said that she had lured them in, especially if he were wearing green, because that was her favorite color.

I kept Norman and Non in the shallows and we watched herons flying overhead and walked where waves tumbled, covering the melted forms of lava flows. Tidal pools were filled with small fish and crabs and mussels, which Norman scooped up in his small hands and studied. Along the cliff walls were narrow caves where fossilized rocks and the remains of small animals and plants covered their surfaces and we touched them with our palms and the tips of our fingers. I put the children down for a nap on the sand and I stroked their hair away from their faces and kissed their warm cheeks and spent the entire time watching them sleep, because just the sight of their faces had the power to mesmerize me even more than the endless crashing waves.

At home, MacLeod was furious. How could you have taken

the children to the sea where the current is so strong! he said, and he grabbed his pipe off the table and chewed on it instead of lighting it and smoking it. I explained to him that we did not go into the water and that no one wore the color green.

What on earth are you talking about? he said.

Green, no one wore it, I said. The goddess of the southern seas would not have been tempted by them even if they had been in the water, they would not have drowned. I was careful, I said. I would never let anything happen to my children. Never, I repeated.

MacLeod did not say anything. He stuffed his pipe with tobacco and lit it and smoked. You're dumber than a child, he said. You believe what the islanders tell you, and you're a grown woman. Are you mad? he said.

Of course I believe the islanders, I said. It's their island, I said. They've learned to live on it.

Don't you see, that's why I'm here, that's why the Dutch are here, because the islanders live on their island like stupid children. They have no idea how rich their island is. They don't even know how to control it. Without us they wouldn't have these large-scale coffee plantations or rice fields or spice markets. Don't you even know why I'm here? he said.

I shook my head. I did not know why we were there. I looked down at my hands and the tops of my feet, which were brown from my day at the shore, and then I sat on the balcony, where a warm perfumed breeze flapped back the hem of my sarong and the warm breeze smelled of lotus, and I knew it was the goddess of the southern seas calling to me from her underwater realm.

A CHILDISH HEART

SHE TOLD the doctor that her heart was skipping. She laughed when she said it, because it sounded like such a youthful thing, a childish thing, and not a thing to do with poor health. Her heart skipping down a street. This time she lowered her gown to her shoulders, so he could listen to her heart. The gas flame in the cell was not bright enough for him. Sister Leonide held a lantern up so he could see better. You are in very good health, he said.

But I'm not, she said. Tell him, Sister, how I worry all the time, how I can't eat my food, how I pace the floor, and how my hair is falling out.

Her hair is falling out, Sister Leonide said, and she brought the lantern to her pillow to show the doctor the black-and-gray S-shaped hairs.

The doctor examined the hairs. He examined her head. He stood above her while she sat on the bed and with his pocketknife he lifted the hairs at her crown. Then he stood in front of her and she looked into his blue eyes while he looked at her temples and her hairline.

Yes, you are losing your hair. This is not uncommon for a woman your age. How old are you again?

Forty-two.

Yes, you are losing your hair. He folded his pocketknife back up.

THE HEAT

AT FIRST I thought I would make friends with the heat. MacLeod and the other officers' wives who had been stationed on the island longer than I had been all said that the heat was what drove them insane. The rain they hated, but it was the heat that made them dream of their homeland and when they were too hot to dream of their own homeland, they dreamed of other people's homelands, and when it was too hot for that, they dreamed of hell and in their dreams it was cooler than Java. My plan was to receive it like a good friend who had come for a long visit.

I even cleaned my house for it. I had new eyelet linen put on all the beds, for the eyelets sounded as if they'd be cool, letting air pass through their holes. I shopped for it. I had cotton shorts made for Norman, and for Non I had small seersucker sundresses made in mint green and slate blue, which would not soak in the heat as much as dark colors would.

When the first days of it came, I greeted it every morning as it streamed in through my window and felt like a branding iron on my bare leg. But like a big dog that panted at my side, the heat did more than follow me. That would have meant I could somehow get in front of it. Instead it mirrored my every move, as if the big panting dog were a well-trained dog, a dog so well trained that it would not leave my side and at times pressed all of its weight into me, leaning on me, making me lose my balance, making me walk into walls and fall down stairs.

I SAW more of MacLeod in the heat. Perhaps the brothel was just too hot and the whores smelled as if they were rotting. At night he slept with his arms akimbo in our bed and in his sleep a hand or an arm of his twitching in a dream would touch me and awaken me. I woke thinking he wanted something from me, there was something he had to tell me, but then I would realize he was fast asleep and there was nothing he had to tell me anyway, just as there was nothing to tell me when we were awake during the day.

I ate in the middle of the night because it was cooler then. I feasted on passion fruit and jackfruit and mango and jamblang and pineapple and rambutan. I ate naked sitting on the balcony (it was too hot for even a sarong), and I listened to the insects thrum while I reached for a plate of all the fruits cut up on a table beside me. Their juices dripped down my chin, onto my breasts, and onto my belly.

Two or three times, when I was on the balcony late at night, I heard a great big crashing from the trees and then a large thud. It was a gibbon, falling out of its tree in its sleep. It was comical to see the gibbon stand unbalanced after the fall, shaking its head, and I would laugh out loud and the gibbon would turn and send a hurt look in my direction and MacLeod would mumble in his sleep and spread his arms and legs even farther out on the eyelet linen so that even if I did want to go back to bed, there would be no room for me.

I slept during the heat of the day in a hammock. Norman

would rock me to sleep in it. Close your eyes, Mama Hari, you take a nap now, he would say. Sometimes Non would sleep beside me in the hammock, curled in the crook of my arm, but when I would awaken she was gone. MacLeod had taken her out, afraid that the hammock would flip in our sleep and she'd be hurt. I always woke from my naps in the hot afternoon feeling that I had a hangover and I had to think back to what I had been doing before the nap. Had I been to a party? Did I drink too much wine? But I had not been to a party. I simply had been awake all night feasting on fruit and listening for gibbons falling out of trees.

TAKING THE WATERS

THERE WAS a coal furnace in Bouchardon's office, which was why she grew to look forward to her meetings with him. She leaned back in the chair, not feeling the need to hunch forward the way she did in her cell where the cold made her feel as if she should withdraw and fold her body around herself to keep her center warm. In Bouchardon's office she set her shoulders back and opened herself up to the heat. She talked for as long as she could, because she wanted to stay as warm as she could for as long as possible. She reminded herself that what she said would have to serve her well, to save her life, but at times she forgot, at times the warmth of the furnace was all she thought about.

I have messages, Bouchardon said. He never showed them to her. He kept them in a folder. Sometimes he would read from them. They were all from the Germans. They were intercepted from the Eiffel Tower.

After the 1889 Paris Exhibition, the French wanted to take the thing down. It was horrible, they said. It was hideous, they said. Mon Dieu, they said. But, they soon learned, it was the highest point in all of Paris and it was ideal for intercepting radio-wired messages.

She did not know how transmissions worked. It was hard for

her to picture words flying through thin air and a Paris structure being able to lasso them and the men inside poring over them, heads bent, decoding them, and wasn't it windy up there? And didn't the slips of paper sometimes sail away from their grasp and float over church spires and rooftops and softly land on the uneven cobblestones where ladies and men and horses even, ground them under the heels and toes of their shoes? The heat was delightful, she thought to herself. The heat is my friend.

Bouchardon read out loud a portion of one of the messages.

Agent H21 of the Intelligence Centralization section of Cologne has arrived here in Spain. She has pretended to accept offers from the French Intelligence services and to carry out trial trips in Belgium for them.

You are Agent H21! Bouchardon said. You are a German spy! You sought out Captain Ladoux of the French Intelligence so that you could pretend to work for him, when really you were employed by Von Kalle, a German officer who sent you five thousand francs for your services, and then you met with him in Spain to supply him with very complete information on a number of political, diplomatic, and military subjects. Agent H21, that is you!

I did not seek out Ladoux to be a spy, I sought him out to secure a pass to go to Vittel, to take the waters. Only to take the waters.

Ladoux said you wanted the pass to go into the war zone to see your Russian lover, Vadime.

Yes, yes, that was the real reason. But I first went to Ladoux for a pass to Vittel for the waters, that's what I told him. Then later, yes, the truth was I wanted to see Vadime!

You have a great deal of difficulty with the truth, don't you, Agent H21?

Yes, no, I am not Agent H21! It's just that it's so hot in here! It's so hot, compared to my cell, who can think in this heat?

MUD FROM THE RIVER

IT WAS WHEN the nights started getting cooler that it happened. MacLeod was asleep on the couch and I was sleeping in my bed. I was dreaming that Prince Rama was my lover and that he had come with his army of monkeys to save me from the evil Ravana. In the dream, the monkeys were screaming as they swooped down through the trees and landed on Ravana's back, attacking him. But then the screams changed. They sounded like my children and I woke up from the dream.

I was annoyed to wake up, I wanted Prince Rama to finish rescuing me, I wanted to go with him to live in the palace. But my children's screams were real.

Running to their room, I collided with MacLeod, our shoulders hitting each other's in the hallway. It was the first time in a long time that we had touched. When I opened the door to Norman and Non's room I thought for a second that they were re-creating some kind of drama. This was a play Norman had watched or been told about by Kidul and the black vomit pouring out their mouths was a stage prop, some sort of black paint they had mixed with spice paste and powders in the kitchen. I was angry with them right away. How could they play like this in the middle of the night when they were supposed to be asleep, and where was Kidul anyway? She should have been there to quiet them down and keep them from waking their father.

It was the smell of the vomit that stopped me for a second so that I stood still in the doorway. It was putrid. It came from deep inside them and then it spouted from their mouths and spilled down their dressing gowns as black as the mud from the river. MacLeod stood still in the doorway too, it took us a few seconds to figure out that they were sick, and then we both ran to them. I ran to Norman and he ran to Non. They writhed with pain in our arms. What happened? I yelled to Norman. But he could not answer. His back would arch and then seconds later he would double over, all the while moving from side to side, reminding me of the way he would roll from side to side when he was angry at me and beat at me with his little fists and I would try to hold him still until his tantrum was over.

Both Non and Norman were screaming and wailing loudly. I called out to MacLeod above their voices as if I were calling out to him above the noise of a raging storm. Get the doctor! I yelled, and then MacLeod called out loudly to me, You go!

No, you! You're faster! I yelled. And then he let go of Non and he ran out of the room. Before he left I caught sight of him and Non's black putrid vomit covering the front of his cotton shirt and I wondered how long it would take the doctor to realize that it wasn't because MacLeod was sick and drunk that he had come to his house.

I picked up Norman and brought him to Non's bed so I could hold them both close. Their heads knocked into each other as they tossed and clutched at their bellies in pain. Their hair was covered with vomit and it hung in long strings from their mouths, which I wiped with my gown. Non was burning up, and she was trying to talk, but I couldn't understand what she was saying. It was because she was so small, and her mouth was so small, that I couldn't understand her words. It was the way it was with all children, I thought, it's not that she's so sick that I can't understand her, I reasoned. Kidul! I yelled. Kidul, come here! But Kidul did not come.

For a second, they were both quiet. Non stopped her feverish talking, and Norman stopped writhing. I could even hear the steady drone of the insects buzzing outside their window. But then Non started again, her vomiting came again and again and she convulsed and I watched how her back, racked with shudders, moved as if some sort of sea monster were coursing through her and in my mind I willed it to come out. I held Norman in my arms. His forehead was cool and he was not vomiting and he was not writhing any longer. I was so relieved. It's passed, I thought, and it was nice to hold him close without his back arching, without feeling his body convulsing.

Dr. Roelfsoemme came rushing into the room wearing bedroom slippers, which I noticed had leaves and grass sticking out from their bottoms from the run to our house. Look, I said to Norman, Dr. Roelfsoemme forgot to put on his shoes! Silly doctor, I said, and I rocked Norman back and forth in my arms.

I need to examine him, you need to let him go, Dr. Roelfsoemme said. I shook my head, and then MacLeod yelled at me.

Let him go! he yelled. But while MacLeod was yelling, Dr. Roelfsoemme was feeling the pulse at Norman's wrist and when he was done, he turned, and said to MacLeod, It's all right, she doesn't have to let him go.

Then Dr. Roelfsoemme went to Non and he started to treat her while she still writhed and cried and he told me to take Norman into the living room and to put him on the couch. I put him on the couch and I lay down next to him and I covered him with my arm and I fell asleep.

When I woke up the heat of the day was coming on and there was a fly buzzing by Norman's head and it would land on his mouth and then on his nostril and I would shoo it away. MacLeod came with a sheet and he told me to get up. I thought how it was probably too hot now for a sheet, that Norman wouldn't get cold with the sun coming on strong, but I got up anyway, and then MacLeod covered all of Norman with the sheet, even his head, and I could see how my boy's face looked like the face of a statue carved in marble, I could see the shape of his nose and the curve of his lip and the angle of his chin through the sheet.

I went to see Non, and Dr. Roelfsoemme was still with her and he was pressing damp towels to her forehead, even though she was sleeping.

She will live, Dr. Roelfsoemme said, and then he said, Do you know who did this?

The goddess of the southern seas? Ravana? The ogre? I shook my head.

What about the servants? Where are they? Dr. Roelfsoemme said.

I walked through the house, calling out to Kidul, calling out to Tekul. I looked under the stairs for Tekul, was he still tapping his hammer on the bamboo steps? I looked in the kitchen for Kidul, was she at the stove frying the nasi goreng? I wished Norman were with me so he could join me in my search. We could hold hands and he would say, Come out, come out, wherever you are! as I looked behind doors and walked the paths in the garden.

I didn't find Kidul. She found me. Her hair was long and loose and tangled. She was standing at the edge of the garden, where the forest began. She would not come any closer to me. Her face was wet, and I thought for a moment how maybe it was raining in the forest even if it was dry in the garden and I was afraid that maybe I had misunderstood the islanders and that the monsoon season came twice a year instead of just once. But it was not rain on her face, it was her tears. She had come even though Tekul had told her not to. She had come to tell the truth, that she had mixed the black poison and fed it to Non and Norman with a teaspoon of gula in their tea.

Mengerti? she said.

No, saya tidak mengerti, I said. I don't understand. You poisoned them? I said.

Ja, she said. And then I pieced together what I thought must have happened. Maybe MacLeod had forced himself on her, and this was his punishment.

I reached out to touch Kidul, but she ran away back through the forest. I never saw her again and I never wanted to see her again.

MacLeod lifted Norman up in his arms and took him out of the house. I watched him walk with Norman down the road, the white sheet trailing in the dirt like a wedding train and MacLeod looked as if he were carrying a cherished new bride across the threshold of their home. It was then that I fell where I was standing, as if the big panting dog from the season of heat was back and knocked me down flat.

I HAVE WALKED across the sea. Constant tides left mud on the flats that were awash with the perfume of violet-headed sea lavender. I breathed in deeply.

*   *   *

Dr. Roelfsoemme was kneeling beside me. I brushed away the vial of smelling salts he had before I realized what was going on. I don't need those, I said. I shook my head. I was still smelling the violet-headed sea lavender.

Over his casket, MacLeod placed the envelope containing Norman's lock of hair, which had curled into the shape of a half-moon. I did not wear black to my boy's funeral. I wore my brightest sarong. The colors were saffron and gold. MacLeod had yelled at me before we gathered at the gravesite. It's all your fault, he yelled. For a second I saw the world as he saw it. I saw the wife he hated that made him go to other women to spend his passion. I saw the servant who deserved what she got, walking around with flowers in her hair and breasts whose brown nipples poked through the silk of cream-colored blouses as she softly carried in a tray or reached with a ladle to serve some sambal.

The first shovel of dirt fell on the envelope, the crumbled bits and small rocks rolled off the white paper and so did the next shovelful and the next and I wondered if the soul of my son did not want his body to be buried at all. If I had had it my way, I would have celebrated his death.

I would have had the gamelan orchestra playing and the wayang kulit puppets acting out his favorite play. I would have laid out brightly colored batik cloths on the ground and placed carved wooden bowls down on them filled with buah and babi and ayam and daging sapi and ikan and sayar, and mie goreng would sit steaming in bowls, the noodles made especially long so that he would have a long life in his next life. He wouldn't be in a box, but on a funeral pyre, where I could still see him. I wanted to still see him, even though he was dead. I stepped down into the grave and put my hand on the casket, thinking I could lift up the lid.

She's fallen in! someone gasped, and then I looked up and there were hands all over me, pulling me up under my arms and taking me away from my boy.

INTOXICATION

THINNED ONCE and thinned twice, those were the soups she was served in her cell. In the thinned-once soup she could see a pea floating here and there and a string of muscle from a cheap cut of meat. In the thinned-twice soup, there was never the occasional pea or meat, there was only a liquid a little darker than water, a little browner. At times her hands shook too much for her to hold the soup spoon without spilling the soup and instead she held the sides of the bowl and lifted it up to her mouth.

I wished they had served me hot water instead because its taste would have been easier to swallow, she said to Sister Leonide. Sister Leonide said she would hold the spoon for her.

I don't mind holding the bowl like an islander sitting cross-legged on a straw mat, sipping his soto and watching off in the distance a herd of banteng down at the river, their hides glowing red in a setting sun and their ankles black and stained with rich mud, she said.

Clunet always sounded hopeful when he came to visit her in her cell. We'll get you out of here soon, ma cherie, he would say, but because he was old and his eyes were always watery, it looked as though he were crying. Sometimes she felt she should comfort him. She patted his arm.

I'm all right. I'm okay, she said to him. He would nod his head. He would stand in the middle of the room and look around, when there was nothing to look at but the stone walls.

BOUCHARDON WAS tapping his pencil and did not look up when she first entered his office. He finally looked up at her after she was seated in a chair. The message I have here states that the Germans knew you were to receive funds from them via your maid, Anna Lintjens.

The Germans could have gone into my hotel room in Spain, they could have opened my letters, they could have easily found the names of people I knew and sent messages that looked like I was working for them. Isn't it called *intoxication*? Isn't that the term used when you want the enemy to believe that one of their spies is also one of yours and so you create evidence that incriminates the spy? she said.

Bouchardon went to the window. He tapped his fingertips on the windowpane. Even the pigeons were used to it and did not fly away startled. Instead they continued cooing and strutting back and forth on the ledge.

Why would they want to do that? he said, stopping his finger tapping to bite off a nail and chew it.

Ladoux asked me to go spy for the French. We decided that I would go to Belgium and renew contacts I had there with German officers, but on the voyage I was stopped at Falmouth. The British took me off the boat, they thought I was a German spy named Clara Benedict. They showed me a photo of her. She wore a Spanish dance costume. She was short and plump. She didn't look like me at all and finally they realized I wasn't her.

But I was not allowed to go on. I had to go to Spain, until further notice that it was all right to go back to France.

You know all this already, she said to Bouchardon. He turned around and looked at her, but he did not nod his head as if he understood. She went on.

In Spain I contacted a German officer named Von Kalle. I'd never met him before, but I had heard about. I thought, If I can't get to Belgium, I will do my work for Ladoux in Spain. I went to Von Kalle's room. I showed a bit of leg. It did not take him long to realize my line of work. He was talkative. He told me about the submarines they were planning to bring into Morocco. We kissed. He told me how he knew the French were parachuting men in behind enemy lines.

Then we made love. It was, perhaps, too easy. But some men are like that, they will tell you things because they are relieved they can at last tell someone to whom it doesn't matter. I have heard stories from men, during the act of coitus, that would make your blood curdle, but I never told those stories to anyone else. That would be bad for business. Then, back at the hotel in Madrid, I told Danvignes, the French colonel, what I had learned from my German, and I told him to wire Ladoux and let him know too. It was a trap, I see now. Von Kalle was just waiting to see how long it took before the news he told me spread. Danvignes even said himself it was old news that Von Kalle had given me. At any rate, it was enough to make Von Kalle suspicious and devise a trap so that you, the French, would think I was really working for the Germans. You would be the ones to do the dirty work and arrest me, they would have to do nothing but send a few messages with false information, and I would be out of their hair.

She stopped talking. She folded her hands in her lap. She thought that surely Bouchardon would see the situation clearly now. It all made sense. The room was delightfully warm again. Bouchardon was silent for so long that she had time to let her mind wander. Was there a way to harness the heat? Could she open up her dress pockets and let the warm air in and then later release it in the cold of her cell? Would just the memory of her being warm be enough to keep her warm when she was sent back with nothing to do but once again sit alone on her sagging cot? Or maybe, this was it, maybe Bouchardon was being silent for so long because he finally understood what she was saying. Maybe she was free to go.

Bouchardon spun on his heel just as she had this thought. He leaned over her and put his hands on the armrest of her chair as if he were about to pick up the chair with her in it. For a moment she thought she was free and he was going to carry her outside. The old leather chair with the armrests was some sort of chariot. She would be held high over the streets. She would breathe in the air of Paris, the petrol from a motorcar's exhaust, the warm sweat of a carriage horse trotting, the perfume of an old woman, the smell of Bouchardon himself, his brilliantine carried up to her in a breeze as he lifted her. Would he call out to all of Paris that she was innocent?

Bouchardon put his face so close to hers that she could see where the bit of nail that he had chewed off lay white and ragged on his lip. But he said nothing to her. He opened the door and told the guard to come and take her back to her cell. She did not rise from her chair right away. What if I didn't? she thought. What if I stayed where I was and refused to go? She closed her eyes for a second and thought of Ameland. What if the water had returned before she finished walking across the sea? She knew the answer. When she finally stood up from the leather chair, her dress felt as heavy as her skirt did that day she walked across the sea. It felt heavy with black silt, deposited over the ages with the never-ending ebb and flow of the tide, only it wasn't the tide that had ebbed and flowed over the seat of the leather chair or the worn wooden boards on Bouchardon's office floor, but the constant ebb and flow of prisoners' answers, washing over the room, lapping up the sides of the walls, clinging to the hem of her skirt and dragging her down. She heard all their answers all at once, prisoners who had been questioned years before by Bouchardon and by whomever had Bouchardon's position before Bouchardon had it. The sound was as loud as a crashing wave. She ran from it. The guard had to run to catch up to her. The rats in the hallway on the way back to her cell were surprised; they did not expect to have someone coming so quickly. They squeaked and crisscrossed in front of her, not sure which way to run with so little time to think about the danger.

TEARS OF EXHAUSTION

BY THE LIGHT of the full moon I went to watch the turtles crawling up from the sea. They came to dig their nests and bury their soft white eggs deep in the sand. Shining in their eyes in the moonlight I could see tears of exhaustion as they dug, and then, when they were finished, they walked back into the waves. I stayed watching them until morning, when the sun rose and I could see the white sandy beaches crumbling down from the cliffsides and the sea that sparkled like crystal and I could see fish in every crashing wave tip as if the water were window glass and the fish caught behind it.

Non was with the new servant when I got back to the house. The new servant looked like a mangrove root. She was gnarled and old and her back had a hump in it that made her stoop and made her always look down at the ground. Even when she was talking to you, she looked down at her feet, not brown but ashen with age, and her toes twisted one over the other and the nails were yellow and long and curving, sharp enough to cut down tall grass in the rice field with one swipe. Her name was Hijau.

Non was short enough that when she looked up she must have been able to see Hijau's face, but I was never able to. I only ever saw the top of her head, the white hair always parted into two long braids that hung down and swung at her sides like white cords of rope.

She was making Non some hot milk and before she handed the cup to Non she went to the living room where MacLeod was seated and she handed it to him to drink. From now on, that's what MacLeod did, he always ate or drank first whatever was given to his daughter. If he wasn't there, I was to drink it first.

It's pointless, I told MacLeod, some poisons could take hours before they killed you. But MacLeod wasn't answering. He hadn't been answering for days now. He would sleep at night by Norman's grave and come back in the morning and drink some coffee and then he would leave again. If I talked to him, or asked him a question, he didn't answer me. Sometimes, though, if he came back early and I was still sleeping, he would come to me and wake me by standing next to me. He would be talking then. He would be saying it was all my fault. He would be cursing. Spittle sometimes shot out from his mouth and landed on my arm or my shoulder or my face.

Hijau and Non would spend hours in the kitchen. Non, because Hijau could not look up, would help Hijau take down the ceramic jars filled with spices and they would wash them and wipe them and dry them and then Non would stand on the chair and put them back up on the shelves. I tried to get Non out of the kitchen. I thought of how my mother had died in the kitchen.

Non, let's go down to the sea, I would say.

No, Papa says the current is too strong, she would say.

Non, let's go into the forest and collect flowers for our hair, I would say.

No, Papa says the leopards will come for me if I do, she would say.

I told MacLeod how I didn't like Hijau always keeping Non in the kitchen. MacLeod answered me then. He said he felt safer when Non was with Hijau than when Non was with me and that if Hijau kept Non busy in the kitchen, then that was fine with him and I was not to take her away from Hijau's side.

ALONG WITH other officers' wives I took a guided trip to a temple. We traveled on horseback up a narrow winding path slippery with scree where if we looked in one direction we could see the rice grass blowing in the wind, and in the other direction the patchwork of a coffee plantation. When we reached the top we could see white mist, the pale color of coconut milk, wrapped like a sash around the base of the mountain. Inside the temple, scenes of the Rama epic were carved into the walls and there were statues of four-armed Siva and his elephant-headed son, the god Ganesh.

In the evening we watched a performance of the Rama ballet. I watched how the other wives watched the women dancers moving gracefully in their sarongs. The dancers' bodies were supple, their long brown arms moved like snakes curling up poles, only there were no poles, just the fetid air coming from the crater where the ogre once threw himself inside and his hideous body continued to burn.

The faces of the other wives grew flush while watching the dancers. None of us had seen women move in that way before.

They moved in ways we could not name and in ways we hoped we could remember later, forever, and we were glad not to name the ways, knowing maybe that naming them would destroy them and, like a pillar of salt, the memory of them might crumble to a pile on the ground if we so much as tried to describe in whispers the ways in which they moved. It seemed as if another sense had been revealed to us that we had not known existed before. There was hearing, vision, smell, touch, taste, and now this, the dance.

When we went back down the mountain in the glow of a pink sunset, our horses sometimes slipped on the scree and hawks above circled for prey below. Anyone observing us would say we, the wives, descended in silence, but really each one of our minds was filled with the notes of the gamelan orchestra and the movements of the dancers.

THIRD EYE

HIJAU CAUGHT HER on her back as she fell off the horse. She had a fever that gave off so much heat that the saddle she used was burning hot, as if it had been left out in the noonday sun. MacLeod, seeing how well Hijau could carry his wife, told Hijau to continue into the house and take her to the bedroom, and he did not make a move to relieve Hijau of her heavy load.

She lay on the bed, tossing her head back and forth, still wearing her riding clothes, which Hijau removed for her while Non peered in at the door, asking Hijau if she wanted help, and Hijau told her to stay back, it could be the work of a naga.

She complained of a headache that was trying to tear her eyes out from the inside. Her fever soaked her sheets so they were as wet as if they had been submerged in water and placed back on the bed and she sat up, glassy-eyed, patting the bed in disbelief, saying the sea was coming to take her and that she could not escape the tide. She ripped off her dressing gown, saying that its hem was an anchor, and she stood naked on the bed looking behind her at the wall and trying to run from it. MacLeod caught her and made her lie back down and he told her to hush, that Non was sleeping, and she swallowed and nodded her head and called him Ganesh.

MacLeod left her with Hijau for the night and he went to the officers' club and walked around the club holding a bottle of whisky and a glass and pouring himself a drink whenever he wanted and later he forgot where he left the glass and he just drank from the bottle instead. He wove in and out of the other officers who were standing in groups and talking and they moved out of his way when he veered toward them and they whispered to one another after he had stumbled past, saying, The poor man, did you know every night he sleeps by his son's grave?

In the morning she tried to peel off the red spots that appeared on her chest in the shape of a bloom that she had only ever seen at night. Hijau gave her milk but she would not drink it and asked for flour instead, thinking she could use it to sprinkle on her chest and make the red spots less red. She clutched at her throat, saying it hurt so much she knew a kris dagger had come for her and she looked for a place to stop the bleeding but there was none and her fingers left marks on her skin that made her look as if she'd been strangled.

MacLeod returned late in the morning with his uniform unbuttoned and wrinkled and blades of grass pasted to his head, adhered by the sweat that had poured forth from his temples while he slept so long by his son's grave in the hot morning sun. It wasn't Dr. Roelfsoemme, the pediatrician, who trailed behind MacLeod but Dr. VanVoort, the doctor who treated the adults. Dr. VanVoort walked behind MacLeod while smoking a cigarette which he stubbed out in the potted palm beside Mata Hari's bed before he examined her. MacLeod excused himself and went to lie on the couch and close his eyes. Dr. VanVoort told Hijau to undress Mata Hari, but Mata Hari grabbed at her dressing gown so that Hijau could not get to the buttons. I have to look at you, Dr. VanVoort said, to know what's wrong.

You're not to look at my breasts, Mata Hari said. They're a sight, you know, my husband tore off the nipples with his teeth, call it passion or rage, it didn't seem to matter at the time and it still doesn't.

You don't know what you're saying, you've got such a high fever, I can feel your heat from where I'm standing, Dr. VanVoort said, and Mata Hari then said, You can start down here, and she slowly lifted up her dressing gown at the ankles until it reached above the first few sets of her ribs. Dr. VanVoort stood next to her and stared from up above at her shapely dark legs and her vagina whose clitoris was not hidden low toward her anus but was positioned up high, so that its orientation was dorsal, and its effect almost ocular, he thought, some sort of slitted eye like that of a snake's pupil, set high like a jewel in a ring that looked as though it could easily be pried off with the right kind of tool.

He had to sit down on the edge of the bed. Do you see it? she asked. Had she meant the eye? He pulled his look from her body to her face to see what she meant. The night bloom, she said. She pointed to a section a few millimeters in width on her skin in the sunken arch formed by her rib cage that was covered with small red spots. He felt relief knowing what those were because he had seen them before, he himself had even had the disease before, whereas he had never seen anything like the body of Mata Hari before.

Typhoid! he said almost gaily.

Hijau had brought in a glass of water for Mata Hari, but Dr. VanVoort took it from her instead and drank it all in one gulp, not realizing the extent of his thirst, and feeling calmer afterward, because of the way in which he drank it like a shot of whisky, so that it had the same effect as a drink of alcohol. He was sure that if the old islander woman who served them could lift her gaze higher and look up rather than down at her bunioned and deformed feet, then she too would be amazed at the vision of Mata Hari naked and it was the old islander woman's severe scoliosis that had kept her mistress's beauty a secret and probably why, Dr. VanVoort thought, her husband was such a wreck, a textbook case of hypertension, what with having to come home to that every night. What man could sleep? What man could get into bed beside her every night and not seek out the hidden glint in her third eye?

He left the house shaking his head, patting his breast pocket for the feel of a possible remaining cigarette inside a packet. When he found one, he thought better of smoking it, the smell of Mata Hari's sex seemed to be on him. He sniffed the sleeve of his shirt and was sure it was there. He felt as if he'd gone to some party as a boy and this was his party favor, his prize to take home. The lingering smell of her sex on his sleeve. He was excited, thinking how easily MacLeod had agreed she must be quarantined, kept away especially from her girl and from him, and Dr. VanVoort felt he had done a smooth job, a very smooth job of suggesting ever so offhandedly that because he could not get the disease again himself that she let her illness run its course at his own coffee plantation, where she could stay at his house and naturally be under his constant medical supervision. Besides, MacLeod, the old bastard, looked as if he could use a rest from his wife's body.

But Dr. VanVoort, on the other hand, was feeling fine and

THE IMAGININGS OF BOUCHARDON

SHE ASKED SISTER LEONIDE to bring her an inkpot, a pen, and some paper. Another letter to your lover? Sister Leonide asked. Mata Hari shook her head. She wrote to Bouchardon. She asked him to stop making her suffer in prison. She told him her cell was driving her mad. She told him again that she was not the German agent H21 and that she had gone to see Von Kalle in Spain because Ladoux wanted her to do intelligence work for the French and she thought she could get information from Von Kalle while she was being held there in Madrid. In the letter she begged Bouchardon to let her go. Then she handed Sister Leonide the letter to give to him.

That's it? That's all you will write for today? Sister Leonide asked. Mata Hari nodded.

Sister Leonide turned to go, and then she turned around to face Mata Hari again.

One thing I learned about people while working as a maid and cleaning up their rooms was that if there were something they were hiding, whether it be money, an expensive ring, or just some writing on a paper, they never hid it as well as they could have, she said. It was as if they didn't want it to be completely hidden, even to them, and that too good a hiding place wasn't always the best hiding place, because even they may forget where it was and it would be as if it never existed at all, which wasn't true. Eventually, I always found it.

I knew if I waited long enough, if I went back to the room every day and looked here and there while they were out, then I would find something. Sometimes it wasn't much that I found, a scarf or a hair comb, but when I found it I could imagine whatever I wanted about the person. He was a murderer and this was the scarf he used to strangle his victims, she was a spy and she dipped the teeth of the comb into invisible ink to write secret messages. You see, it could have been just a kerchief and just a comb, but because the owners chose to hide them, then they were anything I imagined them to be. What you're not telling Bouchardon, Bouchardon is imagining you to be.

Then Sister Leonide nodded to the guard who opened the cell and Sister Leonide left and Mata Hari heard her soft footsteps and the swish of her habit as she turned the corner in the corridor.

AN ACT TO
CLEANSE THE SOUL

THE THING YOU KNOW about invisible ink is that it can be anything. It can be milk, lemon juice even. Write with it and later heat the paper and the words will appear. It's magic. Even sperm can be used as secret ink and is said to be a good one.

What you have in your possession when the French arrest you in your hotel is your bagful of tricks, or so they think. Really it is face powder and lip rouge and hair pomade and Mata Hari cigarettes (yes, that's really what they are called and they are quite aromatic and you have taken to smoking them for their flavor), and also, in your bagful of tricks, you have a Javanese perfume for throwing on the fire and making the room smell like lotus blossoms and an item you had learned about only after your marriage to MacLeod and that was oxycyanide of mercury, which you use as an injection after each coitus to prevent pregnancy. You are in possession of it, along with thousands of other prostitutes and courtesans in Europe, and does it make you all spies?

Guilty, you suppose, of listening before and after and sometimes, yes, even during, to their confessions, their weaknesses, their ills, their complaints about their superiors, their hopes and their dreams and their lies and the lies their wives told, and how they failed their parents and how their parents failed them, and you listen to stories about women they should have loved, but didn't, or women who should have loved them, but didn't, and the listening is always harder than the act of coitus itself and makes you feel more tired afterward, and later, in prison, you smile thinking about it, how it reminds you of what Sister Leonide said, that being a nun was easier than cleaning rooms, and you know what she means, the act of coitus being preferable, being easier than having to listen to what any man has to say and you never understood why the profession was considered dirty, when what it really did was cleanse a man's soul. And who would have thought that in one breath parallels would be drawn between the act of coitus and the profession of being a nun?

You laugh in your cell and for once it is a laugh loud enough to drown out the cries of the prisoners you hear escaping through the spaces in between the stones in the walls and it is loud enough to make the flame of the gaslight flicker and it is not a flicker caused by some miserable draft of cold air barreling through the corridors of the prison, but it is a flicker caused by your laugh, by your breath and your breath alone, and it is a laugh loud enough to keep back the return of the tidewater to the sandbanks of the sea that reached the shores of Ameland.

WHAT A WOMAN CAN DO

HORNBILLS AND MONKEYS screeched down from overhead as Mata Hari slept and Dr. VanVoort drank coffee from beans ground from his own plantation's crop. If he could turn and take his eyes off Mata Hari, then he could see the coffee plants out his glassless window, spanning up toward the side of a hill where the slow loris and the binturong moved through the branches and flowering orchids stirred in quiet breezes as if stroked by the wispy fingers of the spirits who lived in the forest.

As it was, he could not take his eyes off Mata Hari and had not been able to for two whole days and he had sat in a rattan woven chair in the guest room of his house just watching her and occasionally getting up to wipe her forehead with a cloth, or to relieve himself, or to pour himself some more of his coffee.

He had first carried her into the room two days ago and was loathe to set her down on the bed, and wondered if he could not just keep holding her in his arms forever, because while he held her he could feel the skin of her soft arms and the warmth of her fever radiating through her dressing gown and throughout his own body. When he finally did lay her down on the mattress and he was separated from her heat, he felt cold, even though the day had been so hot that the sun felt as if it had been striking his skull, trying to break it open just to quench its insatiable thirst with the viscous fluid from his brain.

He would often go for a few days without food, and so it was not unusual for him to live just by his coffee that he always drank hot and never cold, even on the hottest days, because he believed that heating the coffee released its true flavor from the bean and that cold coffee was something that had never been given a chance to reach its full potential. Which is how he thought of Mata Hari as she lay on his guest bed, her wedding ring misted by her raging fever and bouts of sweating and her body glistening, he knew, because occasionally he would get up from his rattan chair and lift back her dressing gown, placing his palm on the inside of her leg, between her thigh and pubis, checking for, he told himself, her femoral pulse. He was a doctor, after all.

While he held his hand there, he would be aware of her vagina, its wavy folds surrounding her eye-like clitoris, staring up at him on the high perch of her pubic bone. He had to stop himself then from the desire to bend over her and take her in his mouth and feel the warm folds of her on the end of his tongue that he knew he could use to slide between her labia and lick the head of her clitoris and coax out of her tremor upon tremor as her body arched up toward him, positioning and working itself so that the hardness of his mouth pressed against her. He almost wished the typhoid away so that he could take her like that on the bed, but then he feared the day when the symptoms of her illness would fade and finally disappear and he would no longer be able to say that she needed to be quarantined and she would return to MacLeod. He brought her dressing gown back down the length of her body until it rested over her long, thin ankles, whose veins he could see pulsing and in turn quivering the fine threaded weave of her gown's scallop-edged hem.

His coffee now cold, he threw it out the opening of his glassless window. He heard it land on the leaves of the giant hibiscus that bordered the walls of his house. He was going to heat himself another cup, but then he sat back down in his rattan chair and he spread his long legs out in front of him and slid down in the chair so that the back of his neck rested on the chair's ladder-backed top rung and he closed his eyes and slept.

In the morning ants were climbing up his bare ankle, forming a long chain from a gap between the floor and the wall that led to the outside. He brushed them away, so that when they slid off him, some turned on their backs, waving bent limbs. He then took off his thong sandal and got on all fours and with the sandal's sole swatted the ants in a progressive fashion from the leg of his chair all the way to the gap in the floor and the wall where they had entered. Mata Hari propped herself up on the bed and lay on her side watching him and then, surprising him, she said, What are you doing here?

I beg your pardon, he said, this is my home you're in.

No, she said, I meant, here, in Java. Is it for all those plants out there, she said, and she pointed to the rows of coffee plants that she could see from the glassless window.

He stood and put his thong sandal back on his foot and looked out the window she was looking out and nodded his head and said, Yes, I guess it is.

Will you go back someday? she said.

He shook his head. No, he said. I don't think so. I like it too much here, he said.

But you don't like the insects, she said, and she motioned

with her head in the direction of the ants that marched in a line through the gap in the wall and the floor.

Oh, the damn insects, he said. If ever you hear one day that I have gone back, it was because the insects drove me there. They would be the only things to make a man suddenly up and leave a hugely profitable business.

How about a woman, she wouldn't make you leave?

Are you always this talkative after having spent days with a fever that nearly killed you?

I think a woman could make you leave and a woman could make you stay and a woman could take you away and a woman could bring you back. I think that you're that way with women and you've been waiting a long time for a woman, thinking one day one might pop up from out between the leaves of your coffee fields and change your life.

He shook his head and laughed, he rubbed the blond stubble on his chin and was about to say something, and then he stopped himself and laughed again.

Do you like the sea? she asked him.

Yes, he said, smiling.

When I'm better, will you take me there?

Yes, he said, still smiling.

I like you, she said. But I'm so tired right now. I'd like to sleep. When I wake up again, do you think it would be all right if I had some nasi goreng? Can your servant prepare some for me?

No, I have no servants in the house. The only workers are the workers who harvest the coffee beans. I can make you nasi goreng, though. I do all my own cooking.

That's wonderful, she said. Nasi goreng is my favorite dish.

STOPS ON A TRAIN

SHE COULD, if she wanted to, imagine the insides of Bouchardon's stomach—the calcic chips of his fingernails meshed with his noon meal—as he asked about Von Kalle. He kept the decoded messages sent by Von Kalle in a folder. When he held one up, she could see how there were perforations on the side of the slip of paper. It looked more like a train ticket. It probably read *Gare du Nord,* but he said it read that Agent H21 has been instructed on the use of invisible inks but has been reluctant to use them. Bouchardon wanted to know when the Germans gave her invisible ink. Bouchardon had small feet and small shoes and she was looking at them thinking how her shoes were larger than his and maybe this was why Bouchardon was so hard on her, because of the size of her shoes.

I was never given invisible ink, she said.

Bouchardon opened up the file again. There are more messages we intercepted, he said. They all refer to you, Agent H21.

She now pictured the Eiffel Tower like a great strip of fly-paper, with messages floating through the air and becoming stuck to the structure and the decoders having to climb outside and unstick the papers, risking life and limb.

The guard outside the door coughed. He sounded sick. She

wondered if it had something to do with the size of his Adam's apple. It was huge and made his throat look as if the head of a tomahawk were wedged inside it.

The pigeon out the window was the same one from last time. Its beady eyes looked at her and she looked back at it, and thought, Shoo, one interrogator is enough, get back to the park, get back to pecking crumbs off the curb.

There were more messages. Bouchardon was a magician and they multiplied within his folder. He held them up and waved them. Just train tickets. Somme, Besançon, Sauternes, Cambrai—names of places, destinations on the tickets, she was sure.

All proof, he said, that you worked for the Germans. But he could have said, Poof, he could have made the tickets disappear, he was a magician, after all, but he didn't. He said, Proof, and put them back in the folder and snapped it shut.

It was all for that day. Charles, the name of the guard with the tomahawk wedged in his throat, took her elbow as they walked back to her cell.

Any news? she said. News of what? he said. Anything, she said. No, no news that I know of, he said.

When she got back Clunet was in her cell, drowning from the inside out. His eyes were so watery that she handed him her handkerchief so he could dab at them. Instead he held the handkerchief and smelled it, liking the scent of the drops of perfume that still lingered from when she had poured some on it in a hotel months ago.

You're really something, she said, and she took back her handkerchief. Ma cherie, he said. He sat down on her cot.

Make yourself comfortable, she said. He patted a spot beside him on the cot, he wanted her to sit down next to him. Instead she walked to the wall and leaned against it, wondering whose voices she could hear now.

Clunet said that she had received letters from the Hotel Vigo. She owed them 2,000 pesetas. They wanted, por favor, to be paid. The Hotel Vigo, she said. Clunet nodded, it made more water pour from his eyes. Don't do that, she said. Also, there was a bill for a frock whose pocket was repaired and never picked up from the tailor's on rue Balzac. There was a letter from her maid, Anna Lintjens. Bouchardon had already opened it up. It said that Van der Capellen, one of her lovers, had come by the house, asking when she would return from Paris. He missed her and was very sad that he had not heard from her. Anna also said the roof was leaking and that she had had to place pots of water here and there to collect the drops that made a tinny racket in a downpour. Did she want her to call the roofer? Already her horsehair mattress had become soaked, and the house, Anna said, smelled somewhat like a stable. Also, the oven seems to be broken. It doesn't get hot enough, but stays a low temperature. She baked a blueberry pie and it took six hours to cook, but it was good, she added, the blueberries being in season.

A DEER IN THE WOODS

D<small>R</small>. V<small>AN</small>V<small>OORT</small> <small>BROUGHT</small> in the nasi goreng for her when she woke, but her fever had come back and she could not eat it. She sipped some water and then she grabbed at her belly, saying that it ached.

At one point in the day she yelled for Norman to come to her. Dr. VanVoort could hear her yells for her son as he talked to a worker by the base of the hill picking coffee beans. He stopped talking to the worker and ran back to the house. She was standing in the guest room and tears were streaming down her cheeks and she was saying that Norman was dead and then she tried to go out the door and down the hall. Dr. VanVoort put her back in the bed and lay her down and from a dish beside her bed filled with water he wet a cloth and dabbed at her forehead and her chest where the red spots were beginning to fade. He slept beside her that night in the guest bed, wanting to be there if she woke up and tried to leave the house again.

In the middle of the night she woke him up by grabbing onto his thigh. He turned to her, but she was not awake. Her eyes were closed and it looked as though she were dreaming. Nonetheless, her hand so close to his penis excited him so much that he ejaculated. He cursed himself afterward. His pants were wet now. He went to his room to change them. When he came back, she was gone. For a while he just stared at the bed, not believing she was gone. Then he ran through his house calling for her. When he listened for her, all that he could hear was a cricket that had come into the house and was somewhere in the living room. He went outside, still calling her name, and then he saw her in the coffee field. The moon was full and she was dancing for it. He was sure that was what she was doing. He was never able to explain it any other way.

She wore her dressing gown while she danced, but then she started to lift it. She lifted it above her waist and her shoulders and finally above her head and then she let the dressing gown go where it landed at rest on the top leaves of the plants. The way she moved looked to Dr. VanVoort as if there was an invisible cord dangling from the moon and that she was writhing up and twirling around it, trying to ascend it so she could be with the moon. Her dark hair was loose and wave-filled and it hung down to her rear, like a black waterfall. Then she collapsed. She fell and he ran to her and he carried her back to the house and put her back in her bed. He left the dressing gown outside, supported by the leaves of the coffee plants, where it lay as though the form of her body were still inside it.

Her pulse was steady and her fever had abated, but she was weak from lack of food and that, he determined, was the cause of her collapse. He went to his kitchen and cooked for her. He made her soup and, even though she was asleep when he walked into the room with it, he woke her up to drink it.

What were you doing out there? he asked while she sat propped up on pillows and he brought the spoon to her mouth. But she did not even remember that she had left the room and said that her dreams were all of Norman, telling her he was happy where he was.

He told her he wished he had a camera because he would have taken a picture of how beautiful she looked while she was dancing. She said she was glad it hadn't happened at her house, because out in the garden MacLeod might have mistaken her at night for a gibbon and shot her.

Drink, he said, and he made her finish the soup.

While standing out in the field the next day he noticed that the wind had changed and he wondered what it meant. A worker told him it was the spirits in the forest blowing breaths their way because they had planted too close to where they lived. Dr. VanVoort's blond hair lifted in the wind and his gabardine shirt collar lifted also and came up high above his neck to just under his chin. The leaves of the coffee plants shuddered and shook. In his house, the thatch on the roof rustled loudly as if a pack of rats were nesting in it and the glassless windows let in a terrific breeze that knocked over the light rattan chair in the guest room and made the bamboo door bang open and shut, open and shut.

When he walked into her room she was righting the chair. He did not say anything but went straight to the glassless window to bring the woven shutter down and fasten it with a hook. The room was now dark and at first he could not make out anything at all. He blinked his eyes. When he could see, he saw her walking toward him and then she put her hand to his collar and smoothed it down so it lay flat, the way it was meant to. Then she said she was up to some nasi goreng, and the soup he had made was fine, but now she needed something more. She said he'd have to forgive her because she didn't want to go into the kitchen and she explained what she meant when she said she thought the kitchen could kill you. He let the workers go early. The wind was knocking over the woven baskets that held the coffee beans anyway.

He brought a table into the guest room and helped bring her chair to the table as she seated herself. She handed back the fork he had set beside her plate. I won't need one, she said, and she ate with the tips of her fingers. He was going to leave her alone to eat but she made him bring in another chair. I want to hear about your life, she said. He told her all there was to tell. Two fine parents and a younger sister and a dog who once saved their lives from a fire. He was from Holland and skated to school on the canals and was known for having learned how to read while skating and he never looked up while on the ice but always had his nose in a book. One day, yes, he did crash and it was into a doctor who became his friend and it was from him that his interest in science grew and eventually led him to medicine. Women? he asked in answer to her question if there was one in his life. Yes, he said, there was one.

Ah, she said, so that's why you're here. She left you. He took a cigarette out of the pack in his shirt and offered her one. She took it and he lit it for her.

She married another man, he said, so then I thought, I've never been to Indonesia.

And there was a job, she said.

Yes, that's right, he said.

And you thought maybe you could run around in a loincloth all day and have the island girls feed you grapes and who needed that bitch after all, the one who married another man.

He smiled. You talk like your husband, he said.

Do I? That's too bad, she said. Maybe it's the cigarette. I'm not used to talking this way. But my children, I mean my child, isn't here to listen to my language and I don't think I'm offending you. If I am, let me know. Then she reached across the table and took his hand.

Your fingers are stained red, what's that from? she asked.

The cherries from the coffee plants. If you spend all day soaking the cherries in water, they turn everything red. The water, your fingers, your clothes, everything, he said.

I thought it was from a surgery you performed. I thought it was blood.

No, I haven't performed any surgeries lately. Everyone, right now, is remarkably well. There's old Mrs. Dieter, who has rheumatism, but I'm afraid that will never go away. There are a few children with lice, but those are Dr. Roelfsoemme's patients, since he's the pediatrician. I lead a quiet life. It's easy to forget sometimes that I even am a doctor. I can go weeks at a time without having a patient call on me. Knock on wood, he said, and he knocked on a rickety leg of the bamboo table and the table rocked back and forth.

Outside the wind was so strong and the thatch in the roof rustled and shook so much that they both looked up thinking that at any moment the roof would come off and sail out over the coffee plantation. The house had gaps in the walls where the thatch did not completely cover the frame and the wind blew through the gaps and made her shiver.

She climbed back into bed and he brought the cover to just below her chin and then she reached out and put her hands on his shoulders and they looked at each other and he told her how he had come dangerously close to making love to her while she was deathly ill.

I'm better now, is that a problem? she asked. His answer was his kiss. He smelled to her of his Javanese coffee and his French cigarettes and English gin and sea salt and a day at the beach and she remembered what her godfather had said long ago, that children had the sun in their hair, and it was true with this man, she thought. The sun was in his hair, groups of strands were like rays of light. They shimmered and she expected them to feel warm when she ran her hands through them. His eyes were soft brown, the same soft brown as the hide of a deer, she thought, and that's how he seemed, like a deer you were lucky to catch sight of in the woods, but once you moved closer to see, the deer was off, having bolted and running past trees so quickly you could see only the blur of where he once was.

She took off his shirt and saw that his chest was the same brown as his eyes. Later, when he entered her, every thrust he made inside of her she rose up to meet. She felt that the thrust of his hips and his penis were like the steady tumblings of ocean waves, they came one after the other while he pushed and poured himself into her. Outside the wind tore and shredded the leaves of the coffee plants, knocking off clusters of cherries from the vines, and empty woven baskets barreled through the rows and the tall yellow grass flattened as if a hand were pressing it down.

IN NEED OF A PILL

She smelled fish in the prison cell's woolen blanket. She shook it out, the wool a muddy color, its ends grazing the stone floor, but the smell was still there. This is my own smell then that I am smelling, she thought to herself.

It was dark and the gaslight flame was off and there was only moonlight from some sliver of a moon that was so thin it looked more like a curved needle and not anything related to a heavenly body. She wanted the doctor. Dr. Bizard! she yelled. The guard down the corridor came to see her. Charles, she said, How did it happen, your Adam's apple? I mean.

The doctor's asleep, everyone's asleep, he said.

I am not asleep. I can't sleep, she said. Charles shrugged. He swallowed, the tomahawk in his throat moved up and down. Then he said, Did you really dance in the nude?

I'm not going to dance for you, Charles, she said. Go back to sleep, she said. He walked away. She went back under the woolen blanket and pulled it over her head to keep out the sliver of light from the moon.

Dr. Bizard came in the morning.

Where's my radish? she said.

Excuse me? he said.

Nothing, she said. She twirled her hair around her finger, and what it looked like she was doing was using her finger like a gun and pointing it at her head. How are your nerves? he asked. She looked to him as if she hadn't slept, there were no fluid-filled pouches under her eyes. The gravity of sleep hadn't been at work, she had been spared the heaviness of dreams. I need a pill, a lot of pills. I need one for sleeping and I need one for waking up and I need one to keep my food down and one to get it out of me when I visit the lavatory and I need one to stop the ache in my fingers and one to take when I'm sad and one to take when I'm happy, because at times I have been too happy and it scared Sister Leonide and made her wonder how long I could keep this up.

Keep what up, exactly? asked Dr. Bizard. He had long felt there was something different about Mata Hari. True, like the other women prisoners, her hair was dulling, her skin becoming gray like the stone walls, as if she and all the other prisoners were chameleons, taking on the color and the texture of their surroundings. But Mata Hari was different. There was a lengthening about her. A neck that seemed longer, to reach up, to look through the bars of her window. She seemed to stand on tiptoes, ready to race down the prison corridors. Even her hands looked longer than before, her entire body reaching somehow to be free.

Your eyes are really blue, she said. I can't help thinking that it's affecting your vision. Is it better or worse because of the blue? Also, is everything you see a little blue because of them?

I can give you another pill to help you sleep, but that's all, he said.

He listened to her heart again.

It's really not my heart that needs listening to, she said. It's these walls, she said. Go listen, please. He put his stethoscope into his black bag.

Take your pill with water, he said, and he left.

Really, I thought I'd wash it down with a cordial, she said to him as he walked down the corridor and she had her face wedged between the bars. And he smiled, amused by her joke, as he walked away from her cell.

SISTER LEONIDE came in and asked her if she wanted to pray again. No, no, no, no, I do not want to pray, she said. Sister Leonide knelt on the floor by her cot and put her elbows over the woolen blanket and clasped her hands and lowered her forehead over them and started to pray by herself. Do you smell that smell? Mata Hari asked her. Sister Leonide raised her head and looked down at her own hands. They looked more like some kind of intertwined two-handed fist to her, held that way to pound something or to beat something but not held that way to talk to God. She separated her hands and looked at Mata Hari. She liked looking at Mata Hari. She liked looking at her eyebrows. The hairs on them looked as if they had been perfectly combed, but of course they hadn't been, and Sister Leonide wondered, just for a moment, if it was the thoughts one had that determined the pattern and the shape the eyebrows would take. Her own were crosshatched, she thought to herself, as if they were intent on tying themselves into knots, so that sitting in their places would not be a straight band of eye-brow but some balled-up thing, forever unknottable, as tightly wound as a cloth button on a Chinaman's jacket. She'd like to help Mata Hari, she thought. There must be some way to help this woman be set free. Come, she said to Mata Hari, let's write to your daughter.

With some paper and an inkpot and a pen set in front of her, Mata Hari began to write.

Dear Non,

Once upon a time there was a queen who had a bitter quarrel with her son. She forbade him to stay with her and cast him out to the forests. Years later they met again, but they did not recognize each other. Then they became friends and eventually lovers and he asked her to marry him. When the queen learned that he was her son, she was astounded. She knew she could never marry him, so she set before him an impossible task. If between the next sunset and sunrise he could dam up the nearby river, so that the entire area could be turned into a lake, then she would marry him. It's impossible, he'll never be able to do it, she thought. But the prince had some help from the gods, and he almost finished damming up the river. When the queen learned of his progress and that she would have to marry her own son, she had the dam destroyed and flooded the plateau, where her son was then accidentally carried off in the water and drowned. That is how the summit of the Tangkuban Prahu was formed.

Love,
Your Mother

Sister Leonide read the letter. Is there anything else you wanted to say besides that? she asked. Mata Hari took the letter back from Sister Leonide. *PS*, she wrote, *Watch your feet if you go there. They can easily slip into the hidden pockets of hot, bubbling mud.*

Bouchardon reads all the prisoners' letters, Sister Leonide said. He will read this letter too. Write something else. Write something that will make him think you should be set free. Tell your daughter how you wish the two of you could be together again. When Bouchardon reads it he will hear how you are a woman filled with maternal love, that to keep you prisoner here is to keep you from your true nature.

Mata Hari took up her pen again. She wrote, *I know your father has forbidden me from seeing you all these years, but, right now, I would love to have you . . .* Then Mata Hari crossed out what she had just written.

What are you doing? That was perfect! Sister Leonide said.

It wasn't, Mata Hari said. It was wrong. I was going to say I would love to have her here with me. But here? The walls? The rats? The smell? Send it as it is. I have always wanted her to know the story of the queen and her son. Mata Hari then handed the letter to Sister Leonide.

Sister Leonide felt that her eyebrows were as tight as knots again. She was frowning, knowing no way to save Mata Hari. There were no tricks within the folds of her habit, no convincing Scripture in her worn leather Bible that could set the woman free. All that she could think of to tell her was that Bouchardon was a smart man, a very smart man, and that he would know if Mata Hari were withholding anything. Are you keeping information from him? Sister Leonide asked.

There are some things he won't understand and so I cannot tell him, Mata Hari said. If I let certain words come from my mouth, they will act like a boomerang, only not made of ivory or wood, but made of sharpened metal blades, and the words will come back for me, straight for my throat. I'm afraid my own words will kill me, you see, dear Sister. I dare not tell. You understand, don't you?

Sister Leonide shook her head and then smiled. God bless you, she said before she left.

I didn't sneeze. Stop smiling your nun's smile. Give me the cleaning lady's smile instead, said Mata Hari.

BOTH MOTHER AND FATHER

THE NEXT MORNING, Dr. VanVoort and I took a walk together in the coffee field, passing leaves freshly torn whose wet fibers stained our clothes with green streaks. We walked to the edge of the field where the forest began and found bowls of rice that the workers had left as gifts for the evil spirits that had brought the wind so that they would not bring it again. Then we picked up the woven baskets for collecting the coffee cherries, which were lying on their sides in the coffee rows, and we were stacking them when a worker came with a note that he handed to Dr. VanVoort, who handed it to me. It was from Non, a get-well card, a pencil drawing of what seemed to be an endless swirl of concentric circles that I stared at for a while and then held tightly high above the staining leaves of the plants until I got back to the room I was staying in and I hung it on the wall with a pin I had found from a sewing box in a drawer by my bed.

While Dr. VanVoort threaded dry leaves through the thatch roof that had come loose in the wind, I sat in a chair out in the field and drew a sketch for Non of what was around me. I sketched the hillside and the coffee plants and the hut. When Dr. VanVoort came and looked over my shoulder, he asked, Where am I in the picture? And I told him that if MacLeod were to see him in the picture, he might put two and two together and that was a four I did not want to have to explain. If MacLeod found out about Dr. VanVoort, he might never let me see Non again. He might think that because we had only one child left that he could take care of Non by himself. Wouldn't it be easy, he might say to himself, being both mother and father?

KNEE-DEEP IN WINDCHILL

DR. VAN VOORT THOUGHT of ways to keep her at the plantation. Standard incubation was three weeks. He had only a few days left with her. Lie down, he told her. She lay facedown and he felt along her spine and applied pressure to her left and right kidneys, searching for a swollen spleen or organ, any excuse to keep her by his side a little bit longer. But her spleen was not swollen and neither were her kidneys, and examining her and feeling her soft flesh and the curve of her thin waist as it widened to the bones of her hips only made him excited and he turned her over and lay down next to her on his side and started an examination he said she had to endure with her eyes closed. So she did and he slid his hand to her groin and let his thumb find her third eye while his fingers reached deep inside her so that when he was ready to enter her she was so wet that his penis slipped in easily and her orgasm came quickly and then his followed. Afterward he stayed inside her until his penis was once again erect and this time he moved slowly, keeping a rhythm he felt he could keep up forever and that he did keep up even long after he had heard the voices of the workers calling down the rows of the coffee plants to one another, telling one another it was time to stop work and go home.

It was a night neither of them slept. They stayed in each other's arms and watched the moon out the window and the ghost birds flying by, blocking out and then letting in the light of the moon, and Dr. VanVoort talked about what they would do, what could they do? And she smoked another one of his cigarettes and said they were a good bad habit to have and he told her he wished she would work with him on a plan and she told him there was no plan. She didn't like plans, she told him, they reminded her of promises, of things that could never be kept. Plans are too often wrecked or foiled, she said. And that being married to MacLeod meant there could be no plans except the plan to stay alive, and that was a feat in itself.

Dr. VanVoort said he'd be willing to give it all up, and he waved toward the window, meaning his successful coffee plantation, and he said he would take her back to Holland on the next boat out. She pictured herself knee-deep in windchill, muffled and gloved and shod with skates, sailing on ice down the canals with the doctor, red-nosed at her side.

She told him they had to be thankful for the time they had together.

Tripe, that's just tripe, he said, you'll make me colic if you keep talking rot like that, and he got up from the bed and went to the window, but a moment later he came back to her in bed and put his face close to hers and smelled the rosewater she had used earlier to rinse through her hair.

A KNOCK AT THE DOOR

IF YOU DON'T want to become a spy, you can go to the consul of the country you don't want to spy for and tell him, I would like to become a spy. This will result in a brush-off and find you quite possibly on the next scheduled embarkation without any further fanfare back to your native country. But if you are indeed inclined to become a spy, you can tell the government representative of the country that wants you to spy for it and that has sought you out in the dark of the night, knocked on your door, and made you receive him in your see-through dressing gown and silk kimono, that you will spy. But if the representative gives you money and a number of vials with secret inks, you must, the next day, pour the liquid contents of the vials into the slow-moving green water beneath you as you stand on a bridge over a canal. After all, the country the representative is from once held for inspection your traveling trunks on a train from the Swiss Alps to France and lost them and they were filled with ankle-length furs made from beaver and mink and worth more than all the money you made for ten years dancing in breastplates and tights and sporting a veil. Lucky for you, they were gifts from men whose wallets were fat and matched their waistbands and whose belts were so long that when pulled from their loops resembled in length some of the pythons you had seen in the jungles of Java. At least you could say to yourself, when you kept that certain country's money that it paid you for your services as a spy, that the score was now even for the furs that they detained and that you haven't had the chance to wrap around your shoulders or feel softly brushing against your ankles since.

A REMARKABLE RECOVERY

DR. VAN VOORT SLEPT IN the next morning, and when he awoke she was gone. He went out to the field, searching for her, but she was not there as she had been the last time when he watched her dance for the moon. This time it was only the workers who stood in the field, hunched over with cloths wrapped around their heads to soak up their sweat and their backs curved in the shape of cup handles as they picked the cherry clusters from the vine.

He called for her and workers looked up and held their hands above their eyes so they could see him in the bright sunlight. He was walking in and out of the hut, still calling her name, and then he walked a few steps in the direction of the forest, and then stopped and turned, and walked a few steps down the road and then stopped when a worker, still with his back stooped from picking cherry clusters, came to him to tell him that he saw Mata Hari leaving at sunrise. At first it was so misty that the worker did not know who it was. He thought it was the spirit of the forest come to shroud him in his hoary arms and carry him away, but then he realized it was she when she said, Selamat pagi, and so he replied good morning back to her as well before she disappeared down the road.

You let her go? asked Dr. VanVoort, and the worker, with

his head down, nodded, and Dr. VanVoort yelled and told the worker how dangerous that was, just to let a patient get up and go when her illness could easily take a turn for the worse, and Dr. VanVoort, while he was yelling, knew that he was yelling because he was angry that she had left him and that clinically she had made a full and remarkable recovery.

SINDANGLAJA

When I walked into my home, MacLeod wasn't there, and Hijau, because she was stooped and could not lift her head up, had to study my feet for a moment before recognizing me. Non, though, ran into my arms and asked if I had received her card and I told her that I brought it back with me and that I would keep it forever and ever because it reminded me of the water spouts that would sometimes form over the sea. There was a moment when my eyes searched the room and my ears were listening for the signs of Norman and that maybe, really, my illness was a long sort of dream and that Norman's death was a part of that dream. But he did not come running out to see me or show me a new wayang kulit puppet of his, and so I went into their room and the faint smell of their putrid vomit from when they had been poisoned still seemed to linger, held in secret places, in the bamboo window shades where spaces could be seen between the lengths of wood where natural knots prevented tight seals and daylight hovered there. Or it lurked in a mirror's carved frame, wooden roses holding the smell in buds or stored beneath the raised mahogany lips of fluted petals and leaves on climbing vines. The truth rushed back at me with the smell, and I staggered and Hijau had me lean on her and I wondered if all her strength was somehow stored in that hump on her back, because she was able to lead me to my room, bearing most of my weight, and she lay me on the bed and lifted my feet and placed a pillow under my knees.

When MacLeod did come home he stood below the balcony and yelled up to me, asking if whatever the hell illness I had was still catching and I told him of course not and he nodded and then he came in through the front door.

While you were gone, I retired. I no longer work, he said when he came up the stairs.

Retired? I thought. How awful. If MacLeod were retired, then wouldn't I, in effect, be retired too?

MacLeod went on, There's a house in Sindanglaja, high up in the hills. The damn heat will leave me alone there and it's cheap, cheaper than this place. I'll hire a tutor for Non, she won't lack for anything.

But I would lack for things for myself, I thought. I would lack for people my own age to talk with. I would lack for things to do. Sindanglaja was far away from anything. It was far away from the sea and far away from Dr. VanVoort and that, I thought, might be a good thing, but still, a part of me wanted to be close to him. I liked how he would talk about going back to Europe and taking me with him. Maybe what I liked most was when he talked about Europe and I imagined myself there, walking the streets crowded with people and quickening my step, changing from my slow step here, where you had to walk carefully, there were roots of trees carpeting the forest floor, there was the heat you had to listen to, it was always hanging above your head, telling you to slow down, but not in Europe. In Europe, I imagined, there was nothing to trip you on the smooth sidewalk, polished by people, the weight of them making smooth the stone beneath their heels. The heat did not hang close to your ear there, but instead there were winds off rivers, blowing by, hurrying you along.

The move to Sindanglaja had already been organized by MacLeod before he had even told me he was thinking of going there. The next morning movers came to our house and took our furniture. They were not going to move it to the new house in Sindanglaja, that would have been too expensive. MacLeod had already sold the furniture and the movers had come to deliver it to the new owners. I watched them take Norman's small bed from the children's room, and even a box of his toys had been sold. Sticking out of the box was one of his wayang kulit puppets, its head bent backward unnaturally as if its wooden throat had been slit and it was now facing up to the sky. I grabbed it from the box. It was the one thing I wanted to keep that belonged to my boy.

SEASHELL AIR

THE MATA HARI CIGARETTE was advertised as the newest Indian cigarette, satisfying to the most refined taste and made from the best Sumatran and choice Turkish tobacco. One guilder bought a package of one hundred cigarettes.

Dr. Bizard brought a package to her cell. On the package was a dancer who was dressed in a veil, the way Mata Hari dressed for her performances. She offered a cigarette to Dr. Bizard and he lit it and also a cigarette for her from the flame coming from the gaslight. He kept his cigarette hanging from the corner of his lip as he held his stethoscope to her chest, and she shrank back, the metal sound receiver was that cold. The weather had grown bitter. Dr. Bizard apologized. He pulled back the stethoscope and brought it inside his jacket and held it in the pit of his arm beneath his shirt in order to warm it up. After a moment, he said, There, that should do it, and he put the sound receiver back on her chest. Better now? he said.

It's burning me, she answered.

Oh, come on now, Dr. Bizard said, it's just metal.

It's too hot! Mata Hari yelled, and she grabbed the rubber tube of the stethoscope and tore it away from her chest. The force with which she did it pulled one of the earpieces of the stethoscope out of Dr. Bizard's ear and for a moment all he heard was the whooshing sound of quiet air, seashell air, he thought to himself. Ash, too, had fallen to the cot from his cigarette still in his mouth, and he brushed it off and onto the floor. He put his stethoscope back into his bag and then finished his cigarette, blowing the smoke away from her, up toward the direction of the gaslight, where it haloed the flame.

Why don't you dance for me again? he asked her. I think that will make you feel better, he said. There seems to be nothing in my bag that can make you feel better.

She slid Dr. Bizard's woolen scarf from his neck and used it as a veil to show him the veil dance. She did not stay at one end of the cell, as if that were the stage, but instead she circled around Dr. Bizard while she danced, as if, he thought, he were on the stage with her, some sort of prop, an ancient column perhaps, covered in climbing vines, hanging with huge tropical flowers, the petals ribboned with veins larger than those even on the backs of his middle-aged hands. When she was done she laughed a small laugh and said, My arms are weak, they hurt now from having so long not held them up high for longer than it takes me to run a comb through my hair.

THE BUTCHERBIRD

IF YOU WANT to be a dancer, practice for hours holding your arms up high, your hands above your head. Walk that way down the street, sleep that way at night, ride your horse that way, read the paper that way, the paper, of course, spread out on a table. Shake your head at the terrible news printed that day: 144,000 French killed to date. When the zeppelin ships sail overhead and drop their bombs, maintain your pose. You are a dancer. Simply shake your hands of the dust and plaster chips that have fallen down from the cracks newly made in the ceiling. Try not to miss opportunities. Think about incorporating this hand-shaking movement into one of your dances. Sometimes you cannot help yourself, you admire a beautiful horse in a photograph in the paper a German general rides. Remember you must hate the Germans now.

What makes the pigeon fly off the window ledge is not Bouchardon so close to it tapping on the window glass, but your laughter that fills the room. It is like a man's laughter, it shakes the window glass, it heads up toward the ceiling, it causes a pain in the muscles of your abdomen. Call the doctor, you say, laughing even harder. Tears sit in your eyes. You stamp your foot. You are laughing so hard that the tears come loose from their pooled place in your eyes and run down your face. Charles, not sure what the stamping sound is from where he stands outside the door, opens the door to Bouchardon's office even though Bouchardon had not asked him to come in.

Is everything all right, sir? he asks, the tomahawk swinging itself up and down inside his throat with every word.

Come in! you almost shriek. Join the fun. Why stand outside the door and be clueless to the merriment. Bouchardon, you say, Bouchardon thinks I went to a school for spies. Spy school! you say, laughing. Then Bouchardon nods to Charles, a motion to take you away, and Charles helps you out of the chair while you are saying, Imagine, me taking notes, learning from a teacher how to be a spy. Was there a lesson on disguises? Did I wear a fake moustache? you say, turning to ask Bouchardon, but he isn't looking up at you, he is looking at his desk, closing your file.

Charles, you think, is impressed. Your laughter continues down the halls. He feels as if he is escorting one of his drinking friends home from a bar late at night, rather than a woman prisoner back to her cell. There is something he notices that is different about your cell this time. Instead of seeming empty like the other women's cells with just their cot and washbasin to fill the room, your room, he realizes, is filled by the sound of your loud laughter, reaching, he imagines, in between the cracks in the stone walls, your breath a kind of mortar, seeping through and filling the gaps with the warm exhalations of your mirth.

THE BUTCHERBIRD, or shrike, of Indonesia, is known to kill other birds. It will hang its victims on thorns or even wire hooks. Once the victim is hanging there, the butcherbird can use its beak, its feet not being strong enough to break up the meat. The butcherbird is forgetful, though. It will leave its victim hanging there for days sometimes, and you may come upon the sight if you are on your way up toward your new home in Sindanglaja. Years later you may learn that if you say Bouchardon, over and over again, you could be saying, really, instead, Butcherbird, butcherbird, butcherbird, and you are reminded all over again how a dead bird hanging from a sharp broken branch made your daughter scream, which at first you thought was the sound of a shaggy macaque, the one you had just seen, or the long-tailed crested langur, which you had never seen but heard lived nearby.

THE GIBBON

THE TRAIL WE TOOK crossed wide muddy rice paddies that shimmered in the morning sunlight and behind the muddy rice paddies rose the looming shapes of lavender mountains. Underfoot, lizards raced through the underbrush and up and up one of the lavender mountains we climbed until MacLeod stopped in front of us.

We're here, he said. So this was Sindanglaja. First MacLeod checked the house while Non and Hijau and I waited outside in a light bath of pink from a sunset that had just slipped below the horizon. In the house we could hear MacLeod. He was turning over the furniture that came with the house, he was turning over a couch, he was flipping over a mattress, he was pulling out drawers, searching, I knew, for what might be there, crawling or slithering or lying in wait for us.

Non wanted to go in. I want to see the new house, she cried.

MacLeod stuck his head out the window. Not yet, wait, he said, I'm still searching. He lit a lantern. We could see him as he went, the lantern's light traveling from room to room like a restless spirit or a ghost, as if the house were haunted, yet it was the one thing MacLeod could not stomp on and squish with his heel or swat with a rolled-up newspaper or carry outdoors at arm's length on the end of a stick and protect us from because he himself was the ghost.

I did not want to go in. I could have stayed outdoors forever in the cool evening watching the pink sky fade to black, because then the stars seemed to come in, and I felt that was the right way to say it, that the stars came in instead of came out. Like guests coming in through the door, they came in, first slowly, one at a time, and then suddenly all at once they seemed to be there, filling up the room that once was just empty sky.

Finally, MacLeod let us in. The house looked ransacked. It looked as though gibbons had gone through everything. The mattresses he had flipped were half lying on the floor, the drawers were pulled out all the way and lay stacked unevenly on the kitchen countertops, the cupboard doors were flung open, furniture was pushed away from the walls, and it looked as if tables and chairs and the couch were all gravitating together by some unseen force toward the center of the room, where they would do what? Converse? Recount the news of the week?

You clean it up, MacLeod said to me. I'll check the garden, he said.

After I put everything back in its place and Hijau put Non to bed, I hunted through one of my trunks and found one of our hammocks. I went outside and strung it between two trees that had gray spikes growing up and down their trunks, shaped, I thought, like the horns of a rhino. I thought the spikes might protect me, they might just stop a wild babi or a rat or a snake from making its way up to me in my sleep. Before I went to sleep in the hammock, I passed by MacLeod's room. He slept on a bed he had not bothered to make and lay on the striped ticking, still clothed, with a gun by his side, its barrel running down the length of his leg.

In the morning, when the stars were gone, there was nothing to see but mist and I thought for a moment maybe it wasn't mist, but smoke from a fire raging down the hillside and it would be only a matter of time before we would all be burnt alive. When the mist disappeared I could see down below, I could see everywhere. Was that Dr. VanVoort's plantation? I thought. Was that him, even, walking a little sideways, walking as if the ground beneath him were tilted?

When I heard the shot I ran into the house and while I was running I thought, This is it, MacLeod has killed himself because he's realized how depressing it is to be retired. I ran first to Non and told Hijau to keep her in her room. But when I got to the bedroom where MacLeod was, he was grinning.

I got one! he said.

I could see the gibbon from where I was. It was still alive. It held its white hand over its wound on its shoulder and then took its white hand away and looked at the blood that had stained it. Then it looked up into the trees, it looked all around. It looked up at us standing in the window. Its gaze was on me, not on MacLeod.

Kill him, I said. He's in pain.

That was a damn good shot I made, MacLeod said, still grinning.

I grabbed the gun from him. He let me have it easily. He knew I was a bad shot. I was. I shot things by mistake. I shot the trees. I shot the dirt. I shot holes through huge banana leaves and I shot flower blossoms whose petals exploded after the bullets struck and the petals floated in the air before falling to the ground or they sailed off, some sailing in the direction of the gibbon who now had one white hand holding its wound and the other hand on its head, protecting itself, I thought, from the flower petals that were falling from the sky.

MacLeod then took the gun from me and reloaded. He lifted the gun and aimed with one shot to the head, which killed the gibbon.

If you're such a good shot, I said, why didn't your first bullet do what this bullet did?

I didn't shoot to kill, he said.

You meant to watch him die? I said, but I already knew that the answer was yes. It was sport to MacLeod and he took aim again, looking for something else to shoot. He moved the gun from tree to tree, from place to place, from ground to sky, and if the gun were a pen, I thought, the writing would look like Ns and Ws and Ms, written on top of one another, crisscrossing and overlapping, the written language my husband spoke.

THE NESTS OF THE SWIFTS

THE NEXT TIME I saw Dr. VanVoort was when I went back to our old house to pick up the rest of our belongings. A servant named Kulon from Sindanglaja came with me to help. Kulon was walking in and out of the house, taking trips to load what was left. I heard footsteps behind me, and I said, Kulon, take those next, and I pointed to a stack of my folded eyelet linen. There was no voice that answered, only an embrace from behind, and I knew who it was by the smell of his cigarettes and his hair that smelled like the sun was in it, and the faint smell of gin and coffee on his skin. I turned to face him and we kissed and then pulled away. Kulon had come into the room. Kulon took the eyelet linen and Dr. VanVoort said to me, It's time to go.

Where are we going? I asked.

The sea.

But MacLeod is expecting me back tonight.

Will he really be there when you get back tonight? Dr. VanVoort said.

No, I thought to myself. Since we'd been at Sindanglaja, he had quickly found the local brothel, and his days of retirement seemed to stretch out long before him, filled only with lazing about during the day in the cooler air of the mountains and some visits at night with whores to warm his blood.

I told Kulon to wait. I told him if I did not return in a few hours, then he was to meet me at the house in the morning, and that's when we would head back up the lavender mountain and return to Sindanglaja.

Mengerti? I said, wanting to be sure Kulon understood the plan.

Mengerti, Kulon answered, and he nodded and sat against the trunk of a kapok tree, between the roots, which were as high as his shoulders and looked like great gray arms folding around him.

Dr. VanVoort and I took a trail that at first was thin and then it widened and it led over rocky beaches to where rough waves and jagged cliffs raked the sky. On the cliff faces, black flocks of swifts flew in and out over the spray of the pitching waves. Dr. VanVoort told me how the swifts' nests were made, how they were formed by a glutinous mixture of swifts' saliva and hung on the sheer walls of the caves in the cliffs. If one were able to search the bottom of the sea and sift through the sand, one might find the bones of men who had tried to climb the cliffs and enter the caves to capture the nests. Sold for a high price at the market, the nests were a delicacy used to make soup. But some men failed to pick the nests off the cliffs, and they lost their footing, falling into the sea amid the crashing waves.

We walked to a sandy stretch of beach rimmed by coves where angelfish and parrotfish swam in the water but seemed to cease the gentle fluttering of their tails and fins when we came close to watch them. On the smooth shoreline we came across a dead sea snake that had washed up on the sand, its body banded and its head marked with a horseshoe shape on the crown. It didn't bring him much luck, Dr. VanVoort said, meaning the horseshoe on his head, and he picked up the dead sea snake and tossed it into the water.

Have you thought about what we're going to do? Dr. VanVoort said, brushing his hands together, wiping them of sand. Will you come back to Holland with me?

I don't know about Holland, I said. I was thinking about places I hadn't been. I was thinking about France, about Paris, which was supposed to be beautiful. Non would love it there too. The ballet was there. Artists lived there. Great thinkers had come from there. It seemed like a magical place. Even though it didn't have the natural beauty of Java, it had the natural beauty of its architecture and its people, whose minds dashed and darted from one idea to the next, unlike here where the only things that dashed and darted were things underfoot and the people's minds seemed to move as slowly as the fog that hung continually to the base of the mountains.

So you'll do it then, you'll leave him? he asked.

No, I don't think so, I said. I was scared to leave him. Scared that if I did, then he'd never let me have Non, he'd want to keep her from me. He'd arrange it legally so that I'd never see her again, and he would take custody of her, and that was a nightmare I had had one too many times, where I woke in such a sweat that I swear I could have floated away in the salty bath of myself as it pooled beneath my body on the sheets.

A STEW

IF YOU WANT to be a good wife to a bad husband, you sleep with your lover, Dr. VanVoort, one last time and make love on the sand in the dying light while overhead bats as large as foxes fly by. In the morning you wake your servant, Kulon, who has fallen asleep exactly where you left him in the gray roots like arms of the kapok tree and you go on back up the trail to your lavender mountain carting your eyelet linen behind you and two silver salt and pepper shakers, dome-shaped on top, and a fleur-de-lis-framed watercolor painting of a sandy brown castle somewhere on a hill in a Western world. You get back to your husband and you ask him if he's ever been to Paris, and you ask him if he'd like to go. You tell him your daughter would have the best teachers there. You tell him they could drink fine wine instead of the island wine they drink here, which he would sometimes throw across the room in disgust so that it would splash in an arc on the woven mats on the floor. You tell him he's too young to spend the rest of his days in a fog-ridden mountain surrounded by shrieking monyets and hairy-chested white-handed gibbons. You wear him down.

You show him pictures from newspapers you've clipped and

traded with other wives of retired officers whose homes dot this side of the lavender mountains.

Point to the Arc de Triomphe, tap your finger on the flying buttresses of Notre Dame, have him picture himself and their daughter playing hide-and-seek behind trees in the chestnut groves in the Jardin du Luxembourg. Show him pictures of beautiful women, ask him if he's seen the likes of any such women here, on the island, where all the women's skin exudes the cloying smell of nasi goreng and not the smell of fine perfume. Tell him there are conversations with intellectuals he could have there but that he'll never have here if he stays. Tell him how impressed those intellectuals would be with his own clever thoughts, that here they simply fall on the wooden ears of servants and other aging officers falling asleep over their meals, upsetting their soup bowls and staining their shirtfronts.

Ask him to listen for a moment. Ask if he hears the sound of other children, because you know he doesn't. There's no one here for Non to play with. She's in the kitchen again, helping the Hunchback of Java, Hijau, the servant. They're plucking feathers off a freshly killed hen.

Then like the tide, recede a bit. Don't talk of Paris for days. Talk only of the rains that have come. Ask if he can see his hand in front of his face. Ask if his head doesn't hurt from the pounding drops. Ask if his toes and his soles are not itching, his skin waterlogged and flaking, his heels spotted with angry red sores that at night drive him to scratching so hard flecks of blood are left on the sheets in the morning at the foot of the bed. Say you notice he's taken to not wearing shoes. Ask if that's because with the rains his shoes are never dry and every time he puts them on it's like putting on a shoe he's pulled up from the sea. Say he now reminds you of an islander and some day you won't be surprised to catch him in a sarong, eating with his fingers, sitting cross-legged on the floor and dangling a wayang kulit puppet from his fingers, casting a shadow play on a sheet nailed to a bamboo wall. When he tells you to shut up, then shut up. Remind yourself that his head is like a cooking pot and all that you've said is like meat and vegetables and spices, a pinch of this, a pinch of that. He will simmer. He will stew in his own good time. Remember that a watched MacLeod never boils, and walk away.

Don't be surprised when days later, when it is of course still raining, when the dirt at the mountaintop is so loose and drenched that the weight of each raindrop is sending dirt down in great slides, and you think how your house will be next to careen down the lavender mountain, leaving a swath of a slippery trail, when Non is still in the kitchen helping Hijau pound rice, when what could be the sounds of other children playing outdoors is the sound of the monyets and gibbons, a long-tailed lemur—don't be surprised when MacLeod, standing at a window with his back to you, tells you to pack your goddamned things, that you've gotten your way, you bitch.

SOUVENIRS FROM THE ISLAND

My dear sister Louise, wrote MacLeod.

It is with great pleasure that I inform you that we are leaving Java for good and going back home. It will be best for Non. She will be able to have a quality education and playmates her age. If only her brother were going with us too.

We, of course, will stay with you, if that's all right, before we find a place of our own. Margaretha has not been able to keep quiet about moving to Paris and she thinks that's where we will eventually move. I have not told her yet that it is very unlikely I will raise my daughter there and that growing up in The Hague, close to you, is the more ideal and practical solution.

Let me know if there are any souvenirs you desire from the island. We set sail in six weeks.

> *Sincerely,*
> *Your brother Rudolph*

My dear brother,

This is most heartening news! I knew that you would someday come home. I am very much looking forward to seeing Non. I promise you that I will take care of her as if she were my own daughter. You may stay with me as long as you'd like, you have an open invitation. I know that your pension is not a generous one and it would only be prudent of you to try and save money first before renting a place of your own.

As for your wife, I will not whisper a word to her of what your true intentions are. I will play along with your ruse of someday moving to Paris because I know how theatrical and difficult she can be if she doesn't think she is having her way.

As for a souvenir, there is nothing I want from that primitive island that I don't already have here. You and Non will be my souvenirs, so crate and pad yourselves with plenty of straw for the voyage so that you may return to me safely!

Your sister,

Louise

IN NEED OF ROPE

SHE WAS HOT in Bouchardon's office because all of Paris was hot. The Seine, some said, was steaming with the heat, and cats were seen panting, their eyes closed to slits, their chests working hard as they lay trying to keep cool in stone-floored doorways. Bakers cursed, the doughs contrary in the weather, and sunken loaves were thrown out back doors, where gatherings of birds fought for turns pecking. The palm reader was busy. It seemed all that people had the energy to do was sit, but their palms were wet and the palm reader kept a cloth at the ready to keep customers' lines dry and to keep their futures from filling with sweat.

Bouchardon's window was open, but it was the only window in the office and no cross breeze came through. The pigeon wasn't there and she wished it was, thinking its sudden bursts of fluttering wings would create at least some kind of stir in the air. She fanned herself with her hand.

Bouchardon wasn't sweating. He was freshly shaven and his brilliantine liberally applied. She felt sweat sliding down the backs of her knees, and to wipe it away she crossed and recrossed her legs a few times, hoping it wouldn't soak through her skirts and reveal a stain when she finally was told it was time to stand up to leave.

It's cooler in my cell than in here, she said.

Bouchardon smiled. How lucky for you! he said, and then he said, You told Von Kalle information about our men landing behind their lines, did you not?

That was in the paper, everyone knew that, she said. I've told you this already.

Tell me again, Bouchardon said. Tell me why you gave Von Kalle classified Allied information?

It was in the paper. Is information in the paper considered to be classified? Is the weather forecast now classified information? Is the For Sale section considered classified? Is the—

Answer the question.

Because I needed Von Kalle to believe that I was loyal to Germany, not to France. It was the only way he would trust me and it worked. He told me about the submarines in Morocco.

He told you old news.

I did not know it at the time, she said. I hadn't been reading the paper every day, and if I had, it wasn't always the war news I turned to. Besides, when I went to Monsieur Danvignes and told him about the submarines landing in Morocco, he was very excited. It was news to him. That's quite an interesting piece of intelligence you've acquired for France, he said to me. Congratulations, he even said.

No, Bouchardon said, you were trying to trick Danvignes. You purposefully gave him old information because you thought Danvignes would think it was new information, but really it was useless information that all of France already knew about. From the very beginning you were working for the Germans, and therefore you would not divulge any information to Danvignes that was of any military importance or that could weaken Germany's position.

Bouchardon then called for Charles, and Charles escorted her out the door. As they walked down the corridor, she turned to look at Charles, and she caught him just as he was swallowing, and she thought, There, a breeze comes from that Adam's apple of his, that tomahawk moving up and down in his throat. If I had been closer to his neck, she thought, I would have felt it.

TULIPS

THERE IS A TIME when you are traveling on a ship when you wish that you could do so for the rest of your life and you don't want to get off. You just want to be able to stand on deck and feel the wind and be able to always smell the fresh smell of the sea. Then that time passes, and you feel you need to get off the ship right away. You will die if you don't reach down and grab some dirt in your hands soon. You can feel the craving start under your nails, your nails longing for a bit of what could pack beneath them, what could later still be seen when you hold your hands out in front of you. Black moons.

On the ship, MacLeod is sick and Non is playing nurse. She wets a cloth and wipes the vomit from his mouth and then from the ship's rail and the wooden deck. She brings him another coat to wear. She holds the soiled one heaped in a bundle in her arms and heads to the ship's laundry, barely seeing over the bundle in front of her to walk or make her way down steps.

You had tried to help him walk back, but he had flung you aside with one arm and you did not persist and you fell back into a deck chair. Once in the chair, you folded the bottom wings of your coat over the pleated skirts of your dress. You had to keep out the cold.

Later, when you go below to your cabin, you see that Non is sleeping next to MacLeod on your berth. She has her small arm around him and his large hand is covering hers. The other berth in the cabin is Non's, and it is too small for you to sleep in, so you gather up Non's child-size blankets and head back up to the deck. You lie down in the deck chair and cover yourself with Non's blankets that smell of her and the bromeliads you had placed in her hair while at port, waiting to board the ship in Java. You breathe in deeply, not only with your nose but your mouth open, and you think to yourself how what you are really doing is drinking in her smell and you hope you can remember it for the rest of your life.

You watch the moon, wondering if you are sailing by it or it is sailing by you. Maybe, you think, we are in the middle of the sea going nowhere. That is when you feel the longing again beneath the nails of your fingers, the longing for the feel of packed earth and the smell of soil and clay and the feel of grass beneath your feet and the solid feel of the trunk of a tree to lean your back into instead of the dip in the canvas deck chair you lay in where the cloth is sagged and thin, it being a thing to fall into and never be able to heft yourself out of instead of a thing to keep you straight and tall.

THE HAIRCUT

SISTER-IN-LAW, Louise said, what are these? They look like curtains in a bordello. I told her sarongs. I had pulled them out of my trunk. They smelled of the rain and they smelled of bamboo. You'll need wool here, she said. The canals have been choked with ice. You didn't really wear these, did you? she said. Margaretha? she said.

That's all I wore, I said. Louise shook her head.

One morning I walked into the living room and Non was in a chair with a bowl turned upside down on top of her head. There was newspaper spread out on the floor under the chair and Louise was holding a pair of scissors and cutting Non's beautiful, thick long hair short, cutting evenly, right below the lip of the bowl, so that when Louise was finished it looked as if Non's hair was now in the shape of the bowl.

This is much better, Louise said. All that hair was a problem, a nuisance. Riddled with tangles. A chore to wash and rinse. She'll be happier now, said Louise. This is how I wore my hair when I was a girl, she said.

I took Non by the hand and helped her into her coat and we left and walked to the hairdresser. The hairdresser did what she could, she made the bowl shape disappear, but still Non's hair was very short. On the way home she complained of the cold and said she was not used to her hair being gone, that sitting about her neck it had kept her warm, like a scarf.

MacLeod was angry about the money. Louise had already cut the child's hair, why did you spend the money to do it again! You have no sense! he yelled. Louise stood next to her brother and nodded her head at everything he was saying. I told myself it wouldn't be long, that we would be leaving Louise's, that in a few weeks' time we'd be going to Paris.

I thought I could take Non on an excursion. I was the age Non was when I walked across the sea to Ameland. I could take her there. I could let her do it too. Walk across the bare gray flats riven with channels and mud gullies and through the brackish water. Let her see the flocks of terns and godwits wheeling down to feed as the tide retreats. Let her walk knee-deep through the pools of mud the way I did when I was her age. Let her worry when the tide began to rise. Let her think, Will I live? Then safely back on shore she too could say for the rest of her life, I have cheated death. It was a gift I could give her, I thought, a walk to Ameland across the sea.

MacLeod said, No. We could not go. He would never allow it. It was too far for her to go. It was too dangerous a thing for a small girl to do. I did it, I wanted to tell him. But he was not listening. He was pouring himself a drink from a bottle he pulled down from Louise's liquor cabinet. He was shaking his head. Then was not the time to ask him when we'd be going to Paris, but I did ask him.

You fool, was his answer.

Then he beat me, still holding his glass tumbler in his hand, he punched me with the tumbler, on the side of my face, on the bone of my cheek. I fell back against the wall. A painting of Louise's fell down, it was an oil of a windmill and cows grazing on a hillside rimmed with tulips. Tulips were Louise's favorite flowers and she had even planted them in her garden beside the stoop that led to the front door. She had reasoned that if you did not love tulips then you had no business living in the Netherlands. You simply were not Dutch, then, she said, if they were not growing strong and proudly in early spring in front of your house from your garden bed. Then he hit me while I was trying to stand up and I blocked his blows with my arms, holding them above my head, and it was my own arms that I felt were being pounded into me, hurting me. Later Louise wanted an apology, the oil had been her favorite. How could I have been so careless?

The next day MacLeod said he was going to mail a letter. He took Non with him. I gave her a scarf before she went out and draped it over her head and wrapped it around her neck to keep her warm. I'm only going to the post office, Mama, she said. Not Siberia, she said.

That was the time I stood at the window all night waiting for them to come back. I waited with my hand holding the lace curtain aside. I waited even though Louise told me they would not return. It was a plan, some sort of an offensive. Forget it, Louise, your plan won't work, I said.

You were not meant to be a mother anyway, she said. Don't you want what's best for her? she said. You are not best for her. She's happy with her father. She doesn't need you, she said.

Not another one, I thought. Not another child taken from me. I would not let it happen again.

Maybe it was my fault. I should not have wrapped her so warmly. I wrapped her for a long journey, not a jaunt to the post office. I wrapped her for another climate, another country, another life. Louise showed me where the oil was cracked through a cow's loin, the windmill's spinning blade, a tulip's firm petals. Really, she said, if there were anything as valuable in the house as this painting was before you ruined it, I cannot think of it.

I was standing when sunrise came in heavy and gray through the window. My hand was still holding back the lace curtain. While I had been watching the window all night, Louise had packed my trunk for me. Or, more accurately, she threw everything in it for me. My sarongs were all jumbled together, as if they had writhed and slithered over and under one another all night and now lay in a stealthy sort of slumber. Unpredictably they might rise up and strike, an attack of flowered silk and riotous batik dyes upon the grayness of the Dutch morning.

I told you all I know, Louise said. She was strong enough to pull my trunk by its handles down her steps and out the front door. Like her brother, I thought, such strong arms. Before she shut the door on me while I stood outside she said that I owed her for the oil, of course, and that I would notice a pearl strand missing from my velvet pouch. It was a necklace my mother had given me before she died.

All I wanted back was Non. There were lawyers involved. Slick men dressed in newly pressed suits who had time to sit with me in their offices as they sat back in their posh leather chairs and seemed as if they had just returned from holiday or were going on one. Some licked the pad of their thumbs and wiped dirt no one would spot off their shiny black shoes. Some offered me drinks of amber liquor from crystal decanters up on shelves, bordered by thick leather-bound books that looked as though the strength of two men would be needed to take them down.

Some peered over their desks, eyeing my ankles and looking at every part of me except my face when I spoke. Some had me talk to their backs while they looked out their windows at impressive views, swiveling only in their chairs to face me when it was time for me to leave and pay my consultation fee.

I rented a small flat whose windows faced the brick wall of another building so close to mine I could reach out and touch the rough wall with my hand. That was an injustice, I thought, something I did not want to touch being so close to me, and the thing I wanted to reach out and touch, my Non, was so far away. The flat was cold. The room was damp. The wool blankets were as wet and heavy as sponges and I could not use them, they did not keep me warm. Instead I covered myself with my sarongs, because they did not hold the dampness, but neither were they warm, and I shivered in my bed while my teeth chattered. When I finally did fall asleep, I dreamed that Non was dying. There were lesions on her face. Her front teeth were rotten, with holes like windows so I could see through them and into the back of her throat. When I woke from the dream, I was scared to fall back to sleep, I did not want to have the same dream again, and it hovered above me, threatening to come back every time my mind started to drift.

It was the lawyer who looked at my ankles who said he would take my case. I told the ankle lawyer the truth, that I had already sold all my jewelry and that I couldn't pay him, that I had no money. He said there was always something a beautiful woman could use to pay him with. He set up a day and a time for me to return to his office. When that day arrived, I entered his office and he did not say anything to me, he simply took his arm and made a big show of brushing everything off his desk with a grand sweeping motion. The glass lamp, his oversized folders, his papers and pens, crashed to the floor.

He was on top of me and kissing me before I had time even to look up at the tin-tiled ceiling. All I saw was his lined forehead, the lines creasing the flesh deeply, making him look as if the creases were steps. If I wanted to, I imagined, I could just walk right up those steps and walk away from here, but the going would be slippery, the creases were filling with a greasy film of his sweat, but at least, I told myself, I could leave if I wanted to. I didn't leave. When I thought of leaving, I thought how I wouldn't be able to ever get Non back, and then the vision of her I had in the dream came back to me and I knew that I would stay with the ankle lawyer and finish the job. Beneath us, while he worked inside of me, I could hear his desk drawers rattling in their casings and the wood of the desk creaked and moaned, a ship in an angry storm.

When the desk's sides cracked and its top split in two, I found myself inside of it, wedged in between two broken boards that had once been the top of the desk, while the ankle lawyer was still inside of me and a legal pad that had slipped out from one of the drawers was digging into the small of my back. He had to push and pry the broken boards apart as if we had been in a bombing and had to be extricated from the rubble and ruins. After I dressed myself, I asked for more than just my girl back. I asked for money too. I gestured to the caved-in desk. I risked my life for you, I said. I showed him the point of my elbow, which had bruised in the fall.

He gave me money, but it wasn't of much use. I went into the butcher and ordered some chops. Instead of reaching in his case and pulling out the chops to wrap in paper, he handed me the newspaper to read. MacLeod had written a notice in it: *I request all and sundry not to supply goods or services to my estranged wife, who has committed an evil act and deserted me.* I laughed when I read it, because of course I hadn't left him, he'd taken Non away from me instead and wasn't that just like MacLeod to write something absurd, so opposite the truth. The butcher asked me what I thought was so funny and then he told me I could leave his shop. I wasn't welcome. He took his hand and grabbed onto my arm and led me out the door. His hand was cold on my arm, I could feel the coldness even through my coat. There were bits of ground meat on his fingers, which clung to the wool fibers of my sleeve. I noticed them as I stood on the street corner, under a lamp, wondering where to go next.

Louise was home. She did not open the door for me, but she opened the window and spoke to me through it. Non isn't here, and neither is my brother, she said.

Where has he taken her? I asked.

I'll not tell you, Louise said.

I leaned my head back. Non! Non! I yelled up at the windows of the house.

All that yelling and I'll have to call the police, Louise said.

My yelling became a cry, I fell to my knees and I smelled it again. The sick smell of the room that day my boy, Norman, died. The smell was strong, I looked down at my clothes to see if it was coming from me, if my own spittle, my own tears, held the rank smell, but it was not me. I ran from the house, but I returned later that night. I did not knock on the door this time, instead I stayed outside on the plot of grass that was on one side of Louise's stoop. I got down on my hands and knees. Louise's precious tulip bulbs were planted there, they were ready to shoot up their green stems when the frost had passed. I pulled up my sleeves, then I plunged my hands in, and I felt for them. I turned scoopfuls of the black dirt over next to the holes I had dug in my search.

The smell of the black dirt was good. The nails of my fingers seemed to thank me. It was as if there was some kind of transfer of soil through my nails to my blood that was taking place while I dug, and it made me dig harder and deeper, and it fed me somehow. Somewhere inside of me there was a place that needed it. Each time I found a bulb I grabbed it and placed it in a pile. When I was done, when there were no more bulbs left for me to dig up, and Louise's garden looked as if a legion of moles had tunneled through, I left the house holding the tulip bulbs in my skirt. Blocks away I let them roll from my skirt and into the canal water. It was coming on sunrise and I could see how the tulip bulbs at first sank, then later surfaced, and bobbed, cleaner now, a yellower shade, after having washed off in the water. They looked round, like the heads of children, as if the children were in a circle together playing some game I had never seen before. They had no voices, after all, there was no way for me to know.

A BEAR OF A GOD

S͟H͟E͟ C͟L͟U͟N͟G͟ to Sister Leonide's skirts. Don't cry, my dear child, Sister Leonide said. Take strength in God. She asked Mata Hari to get on her knees and pray, to place her clasped hands over the thin, sagging mattress ridden with lice and bedbugs.

Mata Hari would not pray. I have tried praying before, Mata Hari said. I prayed that Bouchardon would set me free, but you see, as well as I can, that I am still here, in this cell, my gray hairs sprouting from the roots, lines beneath my eyes, hanging jowls, the rotten smell of my breath where decay has taken hold of yellowed molars making me sick. The folds of loose skin around my neck create a ring, the jewelry of the aged.

Sister Leonide said she would pray for her if Mata Hari would not pray for herself. Sister Leonide went to her knees, held her clasped hands over the thin mattress. I wouldn't do that if I were you, Mata Hari said, and then she held out her hands and her arms so Sister Leonide could see how bites from bedbugs had left red welts all over her skin. They were grouped in clumps, and then a stray welt could be seen farther away, like a constellation of red stars, mirroring a constellation up above whose name one isn't quite sure of. I never learned them, I don't know, Mata Hari said, all the things in a night sky with names watching over us and I have no idea what they are. Maybe we should pray to them. Isn't there a bear? I could pray to him. To his huge paws, his musky smell, his silver-tipped fur. Isn't he the one really watching over me?

Sister Leonide wondered, before she left, if she could take the silver cross off her neck and give it to Mata Hari, but she knew she couldn't. It was not allowed. A prisoner digging at the stone wall to sharpen the part of the cross where Christ's feet hung nailed through the flesh to the wood could use the cross to slice through the bracelet of bites on her wrists to have the blood spurt and spray the walls, darken the army green blanket with stains in shapes of mountain pools and meadow ponds. God be with you, she said instead, and left Mata Hari alone.

It had been six weeks since Bouchardon had asked to see her. She knew it was a tactic. She thought he wanted her to believe her case had been closed, that there was no more to discuss, unless, of course, she had something to tell him she hadn't already told him and break her silence. Break what? She thought. Stone? Iron bars? She laughed and sat back down on her cot. It bounced with her weight. She made it bounce again. Then again. She laughed. She tried to bounce hard enough to make the cot scrape its bottom springs on the stone floor. Up and down she went. And then she did. She hit bottom.

The force of hitting the stone floor so hard came up and took her breath away. She felt it in her rib cage. It pushed air out of her lungs. She grabbed her chest. Dr. Bizard! She yelled through the bars, holding onto them, curling her fingers around them, feeling how the coolness of the iron felt good against her swollen joints bent on a course to gnarl with age.

Dr. Bizard explained the workings of the heart. There were

valves and chambers she did not care to know. Am I dying? she asked, and wondered if maybe Non would be brought to her. She would lay in the prison hospital, her daughter finally by her side where she could see her and hold her.

You're fine. You're strong, the doctor said.

Yes, that's right. I have walked across the sea, she said to him and told him about Ameland.

He put away his stethoscope. He said he had to leave. She nodded. Yes, of course you are busy. I understand, she said. She stood and walked him the few steps to the door of her cell. Thank you for coming, she said. I feel much better now, she said. Thank you for telling me about blood, about chambers and valves.

It was time for her walk in the courtyard. Charles came to get her. Has Bouchardon asked for me today? she said. Charles shook his head.

There were no more hairs left clinging to the stone walls in the courtyard. There had not been any for weeks now. Whoever the prisoner was must have been freed, she thought. She walked in circles in the hot sun. She thought of the story of how the Indian boy made the tigers run in circles around the tree and they ran so fast and for so long that they turned themselves into butter. I will turn into butter, she thought. Why not? There are already Mata Hari cigarettes and Mata Hari biscuits sold in a tin box, why not Mata Hari butter to spread thickly on toast along with sweet jam? She thought of Non looking down at her in her casket. Her daughter would see not a corpse, but a swimmy gush of liquid lapping up the wooden sides as the pallbearers placed Mata Hari in the ground. Oh, Non, my girl, she thought, Where are you now?

THE BISCUIT TIN

THE MATA HARI BISCUIT TIN had a pretty picture of Mata Hari's face painted on it. Non liked the tin and when the biscuits were finished, she asked Louise if she could have her lunch packed in the tin for school. Louise said she'd rather toss the tin in the trash, but Non begged her and so every day, on the trolley, Non sat with the tin on her lap and looked down at her mother's face. She had no pictures of her mother, and this, besides the pack of Mata Hari cigarettes she was too young to buy, were the only images she had of her. Her father had told Non that since her mother had left the family, he'd had no contact with her, and she had never bothered to write to her daughter or to come see her. Once, though, when Non was younger a woman Non did not know came to pick Non up from school. The woman said she had a gift for Non. It was a beautiful gold watch. Come with me to the train station, and I'll give you the watch, the woman said. But that day MacLeod had decided he would come early to pick his daughter up and he saw the woman.

What do you want? he said.

I have this gift for your daughter, the woman said. It's a gift from the girl's mother.

MacLeod took the watch from the woman's hand and he threw it into the street, where it was smashed under the wheels of an oncoming motorcar. The woman was Anna Lintjens.

THE PLAN

IF YOU WANT to be a kidnapper, don't do the kidnapping yourself but send an accomplice instead. A dear woman who has been your maid in Holland for years, a woman who had heard you crying in the night in your bed as she tiptoed past with clean folded towels stacked in her arms. A woman who washed silk scarves you used in your dances with only a pinch of soap flakes because she knew that anything harsher would fade the bright dyes. A woman who painstakingly sewed small glass beads back onto your costumes after they'd fallen off after a performance and a woman who declared every time you dressed for a performance that you looked beautiful. A woman whose arms you cried in when your letters to your daughter came back unopened, returned by her father. A woman who made you stay in bed when you were sick and who watered the flowers in the garden and who agreed with you that other dancers, Isadora Duncan, for example, did not pass muster or could hold a candle to you. A woman who was tall and thin, with a nose that was as sharp as a blade, and her nostrils such thin slits that you wondered how the air she breathed managed to enter through them and travel the passage to her lungs. A woman who wore her steel gray hair in a bun on the top of her head and used it as a pincushion while sew-ing back the hem on your costume, which she had just sewn the night before. But you had writhed and slid across the marble of the dance floor more than usual, you explained to her, you had undone the hem, yes, but the roaring applause was well worth the cost. She nods her head, pulls a pin from her bun, and weaves it through the folded cloth.

I can smell lilies on this, she says. She lifts the costume up and gently breathes it in.

Yes, you tell her, there were strewn lilies and rare flowers all over the stage and great urns filled with burning incense and can-dlelight and a great bronze statue of the god Siva.

Anna Lintjens shakes her head, the pins staying put, and she smiles. What a life you lead, she says. So different from mine.

But you're like me, you tell her. You remind her how you're both unmarried. She cannot marry because no one wants to marry a woman whose father never came forth to say he was her father, and you can't marry because your lawyers advise you against it. The courts would deem it improper for you to take back Non when you were married to a man other than her father. No, they told you, best you stay single, better yet, too, they say, that you give up this dancing career of yours, and you ask them, If I gave it up, then how would you get paid? How would I have the money to pay for anything? I'd be left for dead on the streets, isn't that right? you say. And they don't answer, they kiss you on the cheeks and leave, patting their breast pockets as they walk out the door, feeling the payment you made them secure on their person.

You show Anna Lintjens pictures of Non. The pictures are

old, from your time in Java. Anna Lintjens puts down her knitting. She puts on her glasses. She sits up straight at a table she's just cleared in order to look. She exclaims.

How lovely, she looks just like you.

You apologize for the photos, for the tattered edges, the fading sepia tone, how even the cheeks of Non are worn where you have touched the face of your girl so many times that her cheeks now look like some sort of white apples no one's ever seen growing from a branch before.

Anna Lintjens, your maid, your accomplice, is the one who has the idea for the watch. She suggests the after-school encounter. The two of you never use the word *kidnapping*, even though you know that's what others would call it. You call it *the plan*.

I will be the one to carry out the plan, she says. You start to tell her no, but she interrupts you.

I'm the person to go, she says. If you went you'd be recognized right away. Someone would contact MacLeod before you could even get a word in edgewise with your daughter, before you had the chance to hustle and bustle her back.

You might be right, you say.

She takes out a pin placed in the bun on the top of her head and inserts it again. Of course I'm right, she says while she does this.

She says she needs to think. She says she will bake a pie, because rolling out dough and crimping a crust is the best way she knows of hatching a plan. The pie is apple. The two of you eat it not after a midday meal or after supper, but you eat it when the light of the day is not yet dark. You eat it when the sun has just gone down, but its light still remains on the earth before darkness falls and you have not yet lit the lamps inside your house.

The apples, with every bite, release a cinnamon syrup that warms your throats, and each bite of the crust crumbles and fills your mouths with the flavor of sweet butter. The pie is a success. You tell her the plan will be also. You both agree, you nod your heads over the crumbs on your dessert plates, scraping with small forks set on their sides the last bits of crust and apple pie filling.

When the plan fails and she comes home crying, the smashed watch held out in her hand to show you, you tell her it's all right. You tell her that you know Non is being well taken care of. You hold up one of your costumes, a halter made of metal to cover your breasts, and you show it to her and you ask her what kind of life you could give Non anyway. Look who I am, you tell her. You shake the metal halter and a jangling sound fills the room. You tell her that MacLeod, despite everything, was always a good father. Then you ask Anna Lintjens how your Non looked.

Just like you, Anna Lintjens answers.

You hold onto the bedpost when she says it, you catch yourself from falling.

THE SACRED TEMPLE

THE DAY AFTER I pulled Louise's tulips from her garden, I saw the ankle lawyer again. This time not in his office but in a hotel I had chosen, whose rooms had gilt-framed mirrors and velvet canopies over the beds. The linens were silk and the beds were so high up off the ground that beneath them, at easy reach, stood velvet-tufted stools to step on when you were getting up or down. I named the price too, and the ankle lawyer paid handsomely.

It was enough for the train fare to Paris and then some. Before I left, I wrote Non a letter, telling her where I had gone, that I would send for her when I could, when I had money. I remembered how Norman used to play with his wayang kulit puppets and imagined how, like one of his puppets, the good puppet, a lawyer working for me would ride on horseback, wielding a kris dagger against MacLeod, driving him away, and still galloping he would sweep Non safely off her feet and carry her back to me. I told Non, in the letter, that I thought that the only place a woman alone could make any money was in Paris. I had high hopes. I would make enough money to pay for an army of lawyers who could bring my daughter back to me.

In Paris there was a series of undressings. I stood in cold garrets, was offered wine in paint-stained metal cups that smelled of turpentine and naked I drank from them. The artist studied. He dabbed, he smeared. I could hear his brush across the canvas. Sometimes he would stop.

The chattering of your teeth is disconcerting, he would say.

I-I-I'm s-s-s-sorry, I would stutter.

Oh, get dressed, he would say.

I was drawn to the smell of horses while passing a riding school one day and I thought I could get a job. I stood beneath a gray stallion whose exhaled breath, like a shaft of light, fell on me and warmed me, and then I sat on his dappled back and rode him in circles in the ring, showing the director, named Molière, all the tricks I had learned as a child, long before Java, long before my mother had died. Molière was impressed.

Get down off that horse, he said. It's your body I like, not your equitation. He told me I had a dancer's body. He made me move on the straw ring, lifting my legs, pointing my toes. Upstaged, the gray stallion was led back to his stall and I had free rein.

After I showed Molière what Javanese women do, dancing the way I had seen them dance at the temple, he said people would pay to see me. In my head I heard the notes of the gamelan orchestra, and Molière said that when I danced I was a body constructed around the articulation of joints, in relation to one another and in terms of alignment and medians.

Do it naked, he said. Yes, he said, while watching me dance naked one day, people would pay through the nose for this, they'd cut off their right arms for this, they'd sell the shirts off their backs for this. You'll be famous, he said. Reinvent yourself, he said, and I did.

I was born in India. My mother was a temple dancer who died

at my birth. I was raised in the temple of a god and consecrated to his service.

Yes, yes, that's it, Molière said. Perfect, he said. Tell me more, he said.

I went on. My dance is a sacred poem, I said. In each movement is a word, and the word is underlined by my music. The temple in which I dance is with me at all times. For I am the temple. All true temple dancers are religious in nature and all explain, in gestures and poses, the rules of the sacred texts.

Molière clapped his hands together. A horse in his stall stomped, banging loose the slats of wood. Bravo! Molière cried, and sent me off. I was ready then for ten years of dancing on stages all over Europe. I was ready for the flowers and the men who sent them and I was ready for the married men who came to me after my performances kneeling on the ground in front of me, their faces pressed against the body stocking I wore, holding my buttocks through the mesh of the cloth, begging for a piece of temple, a bit of religion, a thorough read of my sacred text. What I wasn't ready for was all the years I was not allowed to see Non. The more I worked and danced, the more money I earned to try and get her back, but the more I worked, the more MacLeod's lawyers came with photographs of me wearing my see-through costumes, my breastplates, my navel on display, my pubic hair a matted area of smoky dark behind an opaque bit of silk, reminding me that no judge would ever let me have Non back.

LILIES AND MEN

AFTERWARD, when I returned from my performances and went to my house in Holland, it was Anna Lintjens who washed the mesh stocking, noticing before she soaked it in the water how it smelled of lilies and men. The sudsy water quickly lost its bubbles, the dirt from the floor of the stage and the dirt from cigar-stained groping fingers took their places, showing darkly like the brackish water in a tidal pool at sea.

It was Anna Lintjens who noticed that the rings and necklaces given as gifts by men did not fit in the jewelry box anymore, and she transferred the new jewels into another box, a larger box. Then even more gems went into another box, and then another, and she wondered at what stage it would stop, what would the last box look like? How large would it be?

It was Anna Lintjens who noticed the newspaper reviews and clipped them and placed them on my breakfast plate in the morning so that when I came down the stairs I could read all the wonderful things said about me, about my beauty and my dancing, before I started my day. It was Anna Lintjens who, after I read the reviews, took down the glue pot and pasted them into an album before she started on the dishes and the dusting and the changing of linens.

It was Anna Lintjens who suggested I should dance Salome, that there would be no better dancer who should dance in the Russian ballet.

You've never even seen me dance onstage, I said to Anna.

But I know you would be the best, Anna said while at chores, and she whipped and snapped my blanket in the air before letting it billow and fall perfectly into place on my bed.

Salome, hmm, I said. I looked at myself in the mirror on the dresser, after having to move aside the big box of jewels that was in the way of seeing my reflection. I have walked across the sea, I thought, so why not, I too could play Salome, couldn't I? Anna nodded, as if in response, but then I thought she was probably nodding along with the counting she was doing in her head of the days that had passed since she had last moved the sofa and swept the floor beneath it or ran a damp cloth over the sills of the windows or made a lamb stew.

Now, I said, after Anna asked, Now? Right this moment you want to write to him?

Anna was down on her knees on the carpet looking under the sofa, pulling down a cobweb that spanned from one leg to the next, a hammock of lace, she said, and then I said, "I'll ask Diaghilev himself if I could have the role." So Anna fetched the ink, the pen, the paper, while the sofa sat at a strange angle in the room, still pulled from the wall as it was.

Diaghilev wrote back. The letter was waiting for me on the mantel one day. I opened it before taking off my hat or my coat and still wearing a white rabbit stole strung about my neck. I read the reply, then threw the letter into the flames of the fire that Anna had started earlier, expecting me to be cold when I walked in the door.

He wants me to audition, I said. Me! I said. By now I had performed all over Europe, everyone knew who I was. It was hard to believe he wanted me to dance in front of him in order to give me the role. Anna looked at me. What did she see? My rabbit-fur stole in need of a cleaning, the edges darkened, the fur slightly soiled and in places stuck together, matted by wet weather, a storm spitting drops of ice. My face not yet old but on its way to aging, the lines by my eyes showing white, like tracks formed by branches being dragged across the snow.

It was Anna who noticed I had not slept that night but paced in my room and then came down and stoked the fire in my red silk robe. When the fire was stoked, it glowed brightly like the cloth itself, a burning ember, revived by a flush of air delivered by a poker's iron tip.

Outside the wet weather continued and the drops of ice came in on a slanted wind and hit the window glass with a tick-tick-ticking that sounded as if the house were in the first stages of breaking apart, and soon a rush of creaking timber would be heard and the ceiling joists and corner posts would crack and splinter, bending, the weight of something huge and unseen causing the collapse of my home.

It was Anna who brought me a duvet filled with eiderdown to lay over my lap and a cup of chamomile tea and talked of her life as a child at play in a field full of corn the farmer cut into the shape of a maze she would run through. The corn silk would stick to her hair and her ankles, she said, and there was the sound of other children she could not see, but she heard them navigating through the shaking stalks, the paper talk of the field. Anna smiled, she said she'd like to thank that farmer for his cleverness. It was a gift to her to run carefree like that through a maze made of corn. But of course, she said, that farmer is probably no longer alive.

I told Anna I would do it, if that's what Diaghilev wanted. I would audition after all. By the light of the fire I replied to his reply, and in the morning Anna went to the post office to mail it for me. I waited at home for her to return and I sat drinking coffee and imagining how I would dance Salome, but then my thoughts were interrupted, I kept picturing Non. When we were in Java she had hugged me too hard once, and then she had lifted up her head under my chin. She was little then, maybe only three, and she thought it was funny, but it hurt. I could feel my esophagus becoming bruised, being pushed so hard that I had trouble breathing. I told her to stop, but she continued, so I took her arms off me and I tore her away and threw her down. She fell on the bamboo mat, her elbows hitting hard and scraping on the rough surface. She cried, holding up one of her elbows to show me where it had scraped on an errant piece of bamboo improperly woven into the mat so that it poked sharply through the surface. There were a few drops of blood and more drops of tears falling down her cheeks and then onto the mat, staining it in places. I told her I was sorry, but she wouldn't let me comfort her, she ran through the house calling for her father and when she found him he picked her up and held her and she showed him where she was bleeding on her elbow and he kissed it, his lips turning red from her blood. I wondered then, while drinking my coffee in front of the fire, if Non remembered that incident. I was sorry for days afterward and tried to make it up to her in foolish ways, by taking her for a slice of cake in a bakery in town, by buying her a toy, a doll from England with red hair and a velvet coat. She immediately took off the velvet coat and the plaid skirt and white shirt and bloomers that the doll also wore and she replaced them with a sarong, saying that the doll would be cooler now, in the high, hot sun. The velvet coat and plaid skirt were thrown into Non's bottom dresser drawer, which did not properly close, and months later we found a pile of green bits of shredded cloth inside the drawer where the rats had decided to build their nest out of the velvet coat. Non was happy in Java. It was her home for as long as she could remember and I was the one to blame for taking her away from there and bringing her back to Europe. MacLeod never let her forget that I was the one to blame, and so I reasoned that was why the letters came back unopened. All that I knew was that I wanted to see Non again more than anything. I was lying to myself when I thought that what I wanted more than anything was the role of Salome.

When I auditioned for Diaghilev I think he sensed that. He turned me down and I returned to my home and to Anna and I cried in her arms and she held me and smoothed down my hair and told me Diaghilev was a fool and what did he know. I laughed through my tears when she said it, Diaghilev being as famous as he was and Anna calling him a fool while her hair was swept up in a bun and I could see in it the brightly colored balls that served as heads for the pins she kept there for her sewing.

THE CREAMS MUST GO

ONE MORNING, on my breakfast plate, there was an advertisement cut out from the newspaper that Anna Lintjens had placed there. It was for a cream that you spread on yourself morning and night. You worked it into the skin and it promised to turn back time and change skin that resembled the peel of an orange into skin that resembled the peel of a peach.

The next day I gave Anna some francs. Anna took the money and said she walked in and out of beauty shops, holding the ad, asking for the miracle product. She came home with six jars of the cream and put them on the shelf in the bathroom. That night Anna helped me apply the cream to the folds of skin beneath my shoulder blades.

Anna said she did not know my gentleman friends by name. She did not want to know their names either, she did not know how many there were. She wanted to know only when I would be gone from the house in Holland so that she would not cook more than was needed because she hated to see things go to waste. She did not care to know how the money came into the household. She would deposit the men's checks into the bank and she would keep a record of the balance and handle the checks that needed to be written to my lawyers or, should there be the need, she would take an item of jewelry that one of the men had given to me as a gift and sell it on the spot to the jewelers.

Once, though, a gift from one of my gentlemen did not come in the form of money or jewelry. It came in the form of a horse. I named him Radjah. Anna said that when I returned from one of my rides with him that in my eyes and in Radjah's eyes there was a look that made her think that there was a way to ride to the edge of the world and that Radjah and I had both been there. And Anna said she wished she could go there too someday, and Anna would reach up and place her hand on Radjah's neck, leaving it there a long time and closing her eyes, saying how she had never felt anything so smooth before. Then Anna would gather up my clothes, my shirt and my jodhpurs and my jacket, in her arms and head for the wash, where she would smell them, saying they did not smell to her of men or lilies the way I smelled when I came back from a performance, but that they smelled of Radjah. How I love that horse, she would say. And Anna said she had a confession to make, that sometimes she added no soap flakes at all to the wash bucket so as not to wash off the smell of something she preferred to lilies and men.

Anna did not keep the naked photos of me in the album. There was no reason to keep them, they had brought me only trouble, Anna said, especially the one that my lawyer had showed me once. The courts would deem me an unfit mother without hesitation, the lawyer had said. I would have to spend all my money simply trying to erase those photos from existence if I wanted my Non back.

Unfit, hah, Anna had said. The only un- that my employer is in that picture is undressed. That's a crime? Anna said to the lawyer, who did not answer her, but instead looked at the door as if its wood and its hinges and its brightly polished knob might answer her question instead.

One day I took Radjah to where I thought Non and MacLeod now lived. It was a long ride on the cobblestone streets, and Radjah's step did not falter once and he held his head high. I waited on the corner. Radjah's breath swirled up around me as we stood in the cold and often I leaned over him, my arms around his neck, feeling his warmth. It was a blond woman I didn't know who came out first, followed by MacLeod, who immediately put on his cap to cover his head, which now seemed more bald than ever, and even the remaining hair that he once had on the sides of his head was thinner now and patchy, like a chicken who had had its feathers poorly plucked. On the street, MacLeod walked in front of the woman, and she walked a few steps behind. I was expecting Non to come next out of the building. I was praying for it. If she did, I thought I would gallop toward her and then, what next, I didn't know. Would I be strong enough to lift her up in my arms and set her in front of me on the saddle? How much had she grown? I still pictured her as a young girl and then sometimes the picture of her changed. She was just a baby, running toward me, burying her head in my sarong, moving her head from side to side, saying she could smell sandalwood, her head reaching no higher than my knees.

She did not come out of the building that day. She went in. I didn't even know it, but she must have walked up behind Radjah. Had she, even in passing, touched his glossy hide without me knowing it? It wasn't until she walked up to the stoop that I noticed her. She started up the steps, and her black hair was spread out across her shoulders and it shone even though there was only a weak winter sun. I jumped when I saw her, and

Radjah felt it. He reared as if spooked by a passing motorcar and in the middle of his rearing I spurred him forward and we took off toward her. I was so afraid she would disappear inside and never come out again. She heard Radjah's iron shoes clacking on the cobblestone, sounding more like a team of horses instead of just one. I saw her look at me then, not knowing of course who I was because I was wearing my riding outfit and my helmet. I drew Radjah to a halt in front of her. I was about to speak. I was about to tell her who I was, when from out of the corner of my eye I saw MacLeod. He ran up and opened the front door and shoved Non inside. Then he reached up behind Radjah and landed a slap on his haunch that was so loud it sounded like a clap of thunder and I first looked up at the sky, thinking for an instant that a winter's cold day had turned into a summer's stormy day. Radjah was off on the sidewalk, he didn't know where he was going. He jumped over a baby pram, his heels grazing the covered top. The mother started to scream, but I did not hear her scream for long, I was off around a corner, trying to slow Radjah down. We were long gone in no time. Back at the stable, I realized that Radjah had lost two shoes. The frogs of his hooves were bloody and the end of my riding skirt was speckled like a robin's egg, only the color wasn't blue but red with Radjah's blood, which had spurted up when he galloped across the cobblestones. Anna stayed by his side and lifted his hooves and set them in the lap of her skirt to see how badly he had injured them. Anna, I said, your skirt, and I pointed to show her how Radjah's hooves had left great crumbles of dirt on her skirt, and she shrugged and said how it did not matter to her, what mattered was that Radjah heal, and she brought him buckets filled with ice that she had collected by knocking on the

said. There is no train I can take to go fetch him. There's no gold watch I could offer to entice him. You need to go upstairs and get some rest, Anna then said, and she led me upstairs and helped me change.

Weeks later there was a small dancing engagement at the Metropol in Berlin. I wondered if I should dance the *Chundra* in which I was a young priestess wearing Tamil braids and walking through the garden. Suddenly I notice a beautiful flower representing love. Should I pick the flower? I saw myself dancing, struggling with emotion, then picking the flower and dropping my veil, my body then revealed.

While in Berlin, on the evening before my performance was to begin, I took a walk to the square. There were hundreds of people gathered there. I thought, How lovely, there must be a show of some sort or a concert about to take place. But I was wrong. I learned from someone in the crowd that the war had begun. Then the crowd started to sing Deutschland Über Alles. And the singing was so loud that it felt as if it were coming up through my body and vibrating my blood. I ran away from the crowd, pushing myself past all of the singing people, who never seemed to notice me. Instead their eyes seemed to focus on something in the distance I could not see. For me there was to be no flower picking on the stage of the Metropol. The performance was canceled. War had been declared. On a train I undid my Tamil braids with my fingers as I headed for Paris.

THE ROPE

SISTER LEONIDE CAME IN with consommé. She stood by and watched Mata Hari drink it while Mata Hari sat on her cot.

Isn't there someone who needs saving? Mata Hari said.

You, Sister Leonide said.

Mata Hari shook her head. What I need is a good bath. When I get out of here I'm going to bathe for a week. I don't care if I'm as shriveled as a peach pit when I towel off. Then afterward I'm going to have my hair dyed. What color do you think? Brown like a bear? Black like a raven? Then my nails, of course. A pedicure too. I've got calluses on my feet as hard as the crusts of bread that come from the kitchen here. I feel like I'm walking on stale loaves. Imagine, there was once a time a lover told me he was in love with my feet. He liked to lie head to toe with me in bed so his lip could graze my instep. He was definitely someone who needed saving. I only wish I could remember his name so I could give it to you. He said he'd leave his wife and marry me, but I had had enough of marriage, thanks to MacLeod, and I vowed for a long time never to marry again.

Sister Leonide shook her head. What if you don't get out of here? she asked.

Don't you know, Sister, I will be released from here one way or another. Didn't they teach you that in the convent? Isn't that the whole point? I will be delivered, won't I? Isn't that what you people profess? The hereafter? The pearly gates?

Sister Leonide wanted Mata Hari to fight for her life now. She did not want to have to convince Mata Hari that there was a hereafter, when she had never seen it herself, and she had a feeling Mata Hari would want her to describe it to her. She'd want to know things about it in order to be convinced. What were the flowers like? she imagined Mata Hari asking her, and Sister Leonide would not know the answer. Maybe she would answer instead, You'll be close to God there, and she could see Mata Hari shrugging her shoulders and saying, Yes, but the flowers, tell me, are they like the ones in Indonesia?

Have you told Bouchardon everything? she said.

Jean Riquelme, that was his name, Mata Hari said. He lived in Bailly, who knows if he's still there. Who knows if he still has a thing for feet.

I know Bouchardon, Sister Leonide said. There was a woman here, she had stolen from a family. She had stolen great things, a Grecian urn weighing in the hundreds of kilos made of gold and a huge work of art off the wall with a gilt frame. It was impossible, Bouchardon had told her, that she had stolen these things by herself. Who had helped her? he wanted to know. She told him no one. For weeks she waited in her cell. He did not call for her. Then one day she wrote to him, she told him that yes, she did have an accomplice. Her son helped her. Bouchardon scheduled the trial shortly after that and she was sentenced to only five years. This past month she was set free. She is back home again.

What about her son? Mata Hari said. Where is he?

I don't know. I've never been to the men's side of the prison, Sister Leonide said. But there isn't anyone else you would be incriminating, is there?

No, said Mata Hari, laughing, only more of myself.

Bouchardon hasn't asked to see you in weeks because he knows you're not telling him everything. Tell him, and he'll speed up your trial. You'll be that much closer to seeing Non again.

Again, Mata Hari laughed. I have more of a chance of seeing my Non in here than out there, she said, motioning her head toward her barred window high off the ground. Maybe Bouchardon will call Non in for questioning and she'll be standing in the same room with me and I'll finally have a chance to see her. It's a dream I sometimes have, she said. I reach out to her and she runs to me and we embrace, and from that embrace I know she still loves me.

That could still happen, outside these prison walls, Sister Leonide said, and she brought Mata Hari ink and pen and paper, and Mata Hari wrote to Bouchardon.

Yes, I have some very serious things to say to you. I desire to inform you that I have never attempted the least espionage and I do not have on my conscience the death of any soldier, French or otherwise. I hope that this time I will have the courage to tell you what I have to tell you.

Perhaps the moment had not yet come, until now, and you wouldn't have wanted to believe me, or even admit the possibility of the things which I will tell you now.

Mata Hari sealed the letter and gave it to Sister Leonide. It was only two hours later that Charles then came for Mata Hari and said that Bouchardon would like to see her.

It was still hot. The smell of garbage seemed to come in through the window of Bouchardon's office. She thought she could smell the leaves of rotting lettuce and curdled milk, and maybe the smell kept the pigeons away, because not one was standing on the sill. They were at the Tuileries, she thought. They are flying over the Jardin du Luxembourg. They're on the sill of the Louvre now, staring in at pastels, at the gleaming white marble of a body's perfect form. They're at the Notre Dame, eye to eye with a flying buttress, a gargoyle's chiseled wing.

You have something to tell me? Bouchardon asked her. And she began her story.

In May 1916, late one night, when Anna Lintjens, my maid, was in bed, there was a knock at the door. It was a German consul named Kramer. He said he had once come to one of my performances and thought that because I was fluent in German and French that he could offer me twenty thousand francs to spy for him. I told him I would do it. I had lawyer bills to pay. So Kramer gave me three small flasks. They were numbered one, two, and three. The first and third were white, the second a bluish green. Kramer showed me how the first would be used to dampen the paper, the second to write, the third to efface the text. He told me my code name would be H21. Even as he gave me the inks, I knew I would never use them and I knew I would never spy for him.

Two days later, as my ship sailed through the channel between the port of Amsterdam and the sea, I threw the flasks overboard. I kept the money, though. I felt it was what the Germans owed me for the furs they had kept the time my luggage was delayed on a train trip through the Alps. When I met Von Kalle in Spain, he must have known I had kept the money without keeping my promise to Kramer to spy for Germany. That's probably why he set me up and told me information about the submarines from Morocco, but it was old information and I did not know it. That's why he sent all those messages to Germany in a code he knew the Allies had already broken. The messages said that Agent H21 was receiving money, because he wanted you to believe that I was their agent, I was Agent H21, and he wanted you to believe that I was their spy and that I was to be arrested. Von Kalle wanted me to be punished for accepting the twenty thousand francs from Kramer in Amsterdam and not spying for him in return. I was set up. But I am telling you the truth, I never used those invisible inks. I never spied for Germany. I have told you everything I know now, and now you know why there were messages sent from Von Kalle in a code you could break regarding me, regarding H21. I was afraid to tell you this information earlier. I was afraid it would incriminate me. But I am telling you now, because I realize you are intelligent and that you will be able to see what it is the Germans have done to me.

She stood up then, after she was finished telling Bouchardon her story. Bouchardon wrote some notes on a paper.

I have a request, she said. I'd like to see my daughter, I'd like to see Non, she said.

That's impossible, Bouchardon said.

Why is it impossible?

We don't allow minors in the prison. We never have. You can

understand why, can't you? Do you really want your daughter to see you now, as you are? You should have put your energies into trying to see her instead of spying for the Germans if she was so important to you. By the way, here is your trial date. Bouchardon then held up his legal pad to show her the date he had written there.

TILT AND ADJUST

IF YOU ARE a mourner, you are on the threshold between one phase of life and the next. You must keep your balance as you cross troubled waters. While you hold your head high, experience teaches you that to restore your equilibrium and get through tumultuous days, you need to tilt and adjust, tilt and adjust, that is how you get to firm ground. These are the teachings of Siva.

VADIME

IN PARIS, WHEN I got off the train from Berlin, I contacted Anna Lintjens. I wanted her to wire me money in Paris so I could pay for a hotel while I searched for another performance to dance in. I even went and found Molière. He was with his horses in the ring. There was a lovely woman doing cartwheels across the backs of three horses while she held their reins in her teeth. I could do that, I said to Molière.

No, ma cherie, he said, you could not. This girl is twenty years old, he said while we watched the ends of her hair slap against the bare backs of the horses as she flipped over them and they circled the ring, matching one another's gait stride for stride.

Let me know if you hear of any performances I can dance in, I said to Molière.

Bien sûr, he said, and then he said, Allez, allez, to the twenty-year-old cart-wheeling horse girl and he called her over to him and she came with all three of her horses and they stopped in front of Molière and he raised his hand and motioned for her to bend down close to him and then he reached up and rolled the neckline of her costume down so that more of her breast was revealed.

Okay, he then said, and with a wave he sent her off again to keep circling the ring.

I left and went for coffee down the street, smelling my shirtsleeve while waiting to be served, breathing in deeply the smell of the horses and thinking of Radjah and missing him because I had had to sell him because I was always short on money, and thinking how it was the one time I could remember Anna Lintjens ever being angry with me, the day I sold that horse she too had loved so much.

There was a young gentleman in the café who was dressed in a Russian uniform. He looked at me. His eyes were brown like the soft fur coat of a beaver or a bear, and my eyes, as if they were hands, seemed to be able to feel the softness of his eyes when I looked back at him. They were eyes to fall into, I thought.

His name was Vadime Masloff. He was twenty-one years old. Our conversation was about coffee. Nowhere in France could he find a cup that tasted like what he was used to, and what he was used to was thick grinds layering the bottom of the cup after he had drunk all the liquid and he liked to read shapes in the grinds and imagine that they told the future. If the grinds were thick and piled high, he would have a good day, and if the grinds were loose and spread about like stars in the sky, then he would not have the kind of day he wanted to have. Here, in this country, he said, every last sip of coffee only reveals emptiness, a porcelain reflection of myself.

I smiled at him and laughed because it sounded like what a twenty-one-year-old might sound like and he said he was glad that he could make me smile, because if I hadn't smiled at that moment he wouldn't have known how beautiful I was.

But it's my smile that I like least about my face, I told him, because when I smile my cheeks rise and close my eyes to near slits. He agreed with me but said that it did not matter, one could still see the beauty of the shape of my eyes with the lids nearly closed and that it added much more to my beauty than it took away. I laughed again, thinking again how young he was, and then he said out loud what I was thinking.

You think I'm a boy, don't you?

I nodded.

I believe, he said, that some people age faster than others. I have aged enough in this one year so that it equals ten years. Everyone with me at the Russian front has experienced this too. We are some kind of mortals with a different clock running inside of us. Sure, our skin is smooth, our muscles quick and strong, but our minds, he said . . . and he did not finish. He turned his head and looked out the window, at the street, the cars and carriages passing by. It was then that I noticed his nose. It was straight and long and fine. Like the bow of a ship, I thought, it could slice through waters and leave a wake on either side. I wanted to know this boy, this man.

It was not like other love affairs of mine. He had no money. There was none to leave on my dresser afterward. There was none to fold and tuck into my brassiere. None to be directly sent to my bank account. There were no expensive gifts. No costume jewelry to be added to my giant jewelry box already stuffed with the jewels of others. There were simple gifts. A yellow rose he surely had picked from someone's street-facing garden. The end of the stem torn and not cut by a florist's exacting pair of scissors. There was no other woman, no wife at home, no mistress, no mother still alive to endlessly extol her virtues. There were, however, feverish dreams, and I watched his head on the pillow turning from side to side, and then he would wake and, dripping with sweat that fell onto my chest, onto my breasts and my cheeks and even into my mouth, he would position himself on top of me and hold me down. I wasn't going to go anywhere, but still he held my arms down while he kissed me and while he let his lips touch my breasts, using sometimes just his slight breath to excite me, to raise a nipple to a heightened state in expectation of what was to come next, the entirety of his mouth upon me, the swirling warm wetness of his tongue whose effect I swore was like a cord whose sensation ran from my nipple, through my ribs, all the way down to my groin. It was like an ache, and the only thing that seemed to relieve it was when he finally entered me. He filled me, drove into me while his sweat, which now fell upon me, was not the sweat from some nightmare at the battlefront but was the sweat of our lovemaking.

I told myself he was just a boy, but even my own voice sounded false to me. He was not just a boy, especially not while he had his nightmares.

He was measured during the day. He would rise calmly from my hotel bed, he would place both feet on the floor first and then stand. He would go to the window and pull back the curtain, looking at first at the sky and then down below to whomever was passing on the street. Then he would turn to see if I was awake and he would walk over to kiss me on the forehead, the way a father would. The way my father did in fact when I was a girl. This is no boy, I would say to myself.

You must come look at this sunrise, he might say, and he would help me from the bed and together we would look at the pink dawn stretching in between the tops of buildings and the spires of churches. He would stand behind me while we watched, his hands on my shoulders as if to hold me back from jumping out the window if that were ever an impulse to overtake me.

It was actually my lawyers who advised it and who encouraged it. A marriage, at this time, they said, might help my position. A marriage, in the eyes of the courts, might just be the ticket, the deciding factor, the linchpin of sorts that would get my daughter back for me. How? I asked.

Let's face it, they said, you're getting older. How much longer can you keep up this dancing and this life of being a mistress to other men? A husband now would make you seem stable and respectable. He's asked to marry you, while none of the others have, because they were older and already married. You might jump at this chance.

Will it bring back Non? I asked.

We're not fortune-tellers, they said, we're lawyers. We just hold your fate in our hands, they said, smiling.

Vadime was not the same as MacLeod, I told myself. There would be no drunken nights and then the days where I would find MacLeod baking in the sun, still wearing his uniform but open now, the wobbly brass buttons hanging by a thread, dulled with scratches from scraping on the rocks after falling facedown in the road. There would be no explaining to Non that her father was sick, had taken ill, a fever, a flu, and that he needed rest and quiet. She would come to his bedside and sing for him a song she knew to sleep by, but MacLeod, hungover, with a splitting head that felt as if it had been cut in half with the cleaver that stooped-over Hijau had kept in the kitchen and used for cutting the heads off chickens, did not want to hear singing. Get her out, get her the goddamned hell out of the room! he would say. I would take Non by the shoulders then and steer her out of the room and into the living room and out to the garden.

She would sit in my lap and play a clapping game and she showed me one where you start the game by first clapping your own chest, your arms crossed, and then you clap each other's hands and Non said, That is the way they put Norman in the box when he died, with his arms crossed, and so she called it the Norm game and I tried to teach her other clapping games because Non was right, it was the way they had laid my boy in the coffin and I could not bear to see Non with her own slender arms crossed over her chest in the same position, but Non did not want to play another game. And so, while MacLeod snored above me, reeking in our bed, the sweat pouring out of him rancid with sweet alcohol on the eyelet sheets, we played the dead Norm game over and over again.

FROSTED LEAVES

WHILE IN BED with Vadime in the morning I heard the gentle thud of the hotel maid leaving the paper outside the door. I knew it lay there with the news of the western front, how the Germans behind the Hindenburg Line were destroying towns, villages, and means of communication. They were cutting down forests and poisoning water supplies. I stroked Vadime where on his forehead a jagged stretch of vein pulsed regularly. Oh, God, I prayed, protect this one.

When he woke he said he must go back to the front, his leave was now over. He put on his khaki uniform while I watched him from bed. He put on his papakha, his sheepskin winter hat with the oval cockade in the Romanov colors stitched in the center. When he bent down to kiss me he did not stop and it turned into him stretching out on top of me and unbuttoning his trousers and releasing himself from them. He entered me that way, without even taking off his trousers but just unbuttoning them. Neither did he unbuckle his engraved brass belt. While he was inside of me I noticed the smell of some kind of lanolin or oil worked into the sheepskin of his papakha. It was mixed in with the smell of the sweat from his smooth, unlined brow. Later, when he left, he called me his bride, even though we would not be married for weeks. He closed the door and I looked down at myself and noticed how the buckle of his engraved brass belt had gouged my skin, leaving a mark, as if I'd been branded.

I received a letter from Anna Lintjens at my hotel. Van der Capellen, one of my Dutch gentlemen, had sent Anna his usual modest monthly check to help pay for my expenses. Did I want to use part of the money to hire painters to paint the trim? It was becoming cracked, Anna wrote, and flecks of it fell into the garden and peppered the frosted leaves of the plants. I wrote her back, saying not to spend the money on the house. I was to get married to Vadime and we would need the money for the wedding and I would need money, of course, to keep paying my lawyers. We would need all the money I could make between now and then, in fact.

Send me all of my calling cards from the top drawer in my bureau, I wrote. While I'm here in Paris I can contact a number of gentlemen. Send Ambassador Jules Cambon's card. Remember Monseigneur Messimy, the ministry of war? Be sure to send his address as well. He was always generous, especially when his wife was out of town. Let's hope she's taken a respite from this war and gone to visit relatives elsewhere.

Here the streets seem to be filled with the smell of shoe polish coming from the shoe-polish stands, they are working hard these days, the men who polish shoes, because everywhere you look there are men in uniforms whose boots are so well shined they could serve as mirrors and I can see the hems of my skirts reflected in them. The smell of polish even overwhelms sometimes the sweet smell coming from the patisseries and I am not experiencing my usual love of Paris at the moment, but I am finding it a grayer place to be, as if the smoke from all the guns at the front has formed a cloud and drifted here and settled itself between the cobblestones and the sky.

Then I also received a letter from Vadime from a hospital at the front.

The same mud we curse all the time, he wrote, *the same mud we stagger in and slip in and that yanks off our boots every time we take a step is the mud that saved me. The Germans had been firing down shells that landed on corpses already torn to shreds and the shells kept shredding the rotting flesh into even smaller bits, over and over again, and then a shell exploded near me. Shrapnel flew into my eyes, and I sank down to hide in one gaping shell hole of this corpse-filled mud. I thought I would drown and I could not see. I swallowed, I could not help it, mouthfuls of water putrid with rotten flesh and scraps of men's bodies, and I tried to scream. Then I was saved, I was pulled out of the wretched mess, but one eye is damaged and I may lose sight in the other one. Dear Mata, can't you find a way to come see me? I need you here. Will you still love me if I become completely blind?*

The moment I finished reading his letter, a darkness fell over the city. A second ago it had been daylight, the next moment it was dark, and I could only imagine that it was really from some giant plane flying overhead whose tremendous size no one had seen before and whose vast underbelly created a shadow over the entire city. But that was not the case, it was only a sudden shift in light.

I could not sleep that night but held Vadime's letter in my hand while I sat in a chair, looking out my hotel window at the starless sky and praying that he would be safe. I wasn't sure whom I prayed to, was it to Siva or to God? I remember I named the names of saints I hadn't named since I was a girl and a rosary spilled from my lips as if it were an uncontrollable tremble that seemed to have been held there all these years for some sort of safekeeping and was now finally allowed to break forth and it did with the force and urgency of water held behind a broken flood wall.

After that is when I went to the French police and found Captain Ladoux. I asked him for a week's pass to go and visit Vadime and he took me by surprise and he asked me to spy for France in return. The payment I would receive from France, I learned, could be as high as 1 million francs. With that kind of money I dreamed of being able to marry Vadime properly and to support both him and Non. The courts would allow her to come and live with me because I would have created such a secure and lovely home for her to live in with a stepfather who would care for her and a well-tended house. Most importantly, she would be with me, her mother, and couldn't the courts see that was all that could possibly matter?

In Vittel, I rented a room for Vadime and myself. I closed the shutters. I kept out the sunlight and left the lamp low. It was all for his eyes. Our meals were brought to us. He looked at himself in the silver lid of the tray that covered our dinner. He wanted to see how he looked. The swelling's gone down, I said.

I wonder if I'll lose sight in this eye too, he said, and he touched his fingertip to one of his eyebrows to show me which eye he meant. Then he said, Sit here, and I sat next to him on the bed and he looked at me for what could have been almost an hour. He said he wanted to be able to remember exactly the way that I looked just in case he did go totally blind in both eyes. I laughed, I said we might make a good couple after all considering that if he were blind he wouldn't be able to see me age into a wrinkled old woman and maybe, just maybe, he would never leave me for a younger woman.

That night we made love. At first he lay on his back, to lessen the pain of injury to his eyes, but then his eyes didn't seem to matter to him, he did not mind the pain, he said, and he lay on top of me and covered me completely. By this I mean he stretched out my arms and his arms covered mine, right to my fingertips being covered by his and his legs covered my legs and he clung to me like a shadow, and I thought how if someone were to see us from up above, then all that one could see would be him. I was no longer visible.

THE GIRL

ANNA LINTJENS was dusting. She feather-dusted the lampshade by Mata Hari's bed. She dusted the jewelry box on Mata Hari's chest of drawers. The jewelry box was almost as long and wide as the top of the chest of drawers was. It was a box Mata Hari had brought back from a trip she had taken to Egypt. She had gone for ideas. She needed ideas for new dances that might re-kindle her fame. All that she brought back was the box. Its cover was bordered with sanded bone and its center inlaid with bits of mother-of-pearl. Anna thought how it would probably be the last box. There would be no gifts of jewels now. There would be no reason to find a bigger box now that Mata Hari was going to marry a man who served at the front and who was not rich and whose gifts would be his endearments and his outpourings of love. Anna thought to herself how she might like this young man. She wondered what he liked to eat, what was his favorite meal, and she made a note to herself to ask the neighbor down the way whose parents had been Russian if she knew of any reci-pes from her village that she could cook for the young man that he might like. She pictured holidays with him, laying out a plate of caviar and crackers on the mantel and a decanter of vodka while they ate and drank and watched candle flames flicker on the Christmas tree he had helped to carry through the streets to their home.

Anna went to the window. She feather-dusted the curtains. When she looked out the window she noticed a young girl walking on the street below. The girl had thick black hair, as thick as Mata Hari's hair once was. The girl stopped and looked up at Mata Hari's house and then the girl walked on. Anna was sure it was Non.

VON KALLE

AFTER I RETURNED from seeing Vadime, I met with Ladoux again. We decided that I should set out for Belgium via Falmouth, so that I could renew contacts with enlisted Germans I had known in Belgium who were posted there. I thought there might be a chance that I could obtain information from them. However, I did not get far. When I had left France and was ready to depart for Falmouth, a British officer took me by the arm. At first I thought he might be helping me to board the ship, but then something about his grip on my arm, which I felt clear to the bone, and the way he steered me on the quay made me realize he was not trying to make my acquaintance or to aid a lady traveling alone.

I was brought to the police station. Are you German Agent AF44? they asked me.

Of course not, I said. Then an officer produced a picture of a dancer in a Spanish dress with a white mantilla. She was carrying a fan in her right hand and had her left hand on her hip.

That's you, the officer said. You are Clara Benedict.

I shook my head. No, that is certainly not I.

Yes, yes, the officer said. You are a dancer. She is a dancer.

You are German Agent AF44. He was a thin man, this officer. His fingers were also long and thin and pale, and I thought how they looked like a group of white snakes I had once seen writhing on the forest floor in Sindanglaja. He touched me with his hand and made me turn to look at the photograph again, and I quickly stood up and moved away from him. The mist had clung low to the forest floor the day I saw the white snakes and it was getting dark and I was afraid I would twist on a root and fall on top of the snakes as I tried to cross their path and I did not know what kind of white snakes they were. I could not remember Tekul ever telling me about white snakes, and they could only ever be evil, I thought, what with their eyes so red and their skin so pale and as they twisted and turned around one another I could see through to their organs, the blood blue in their veins as they offered up their underbellies to the on-coming night.

I was sent to Scotland Yard, where a man named Sir Basil Thompson, assistant commissioner of police, took only a moment to realize I wasn't AF44, a.k.a. Clara Benedict. No, certainly not, he said looking at the picture the officer with the white snake fingers showed him. This woman in the picture's much shorter than you, he said. He turned to me with eyes that drooped as if when he was a child he had held the pockets of skin beneath his eyes down with his fingers making silly faces all day and they had sagged that way forever, and he said, My dear lady, who are you?

I told him that I was working for Ladoux in Paris and that he should telegraph Ladoux who would confirm what I'd said. Thompson did telegraph Ladoux and Ladoux wrote back. His message said: *I understand nothing, send her to Spain.* And so I was sent to Madrid, not knowing why I had been sent there and not knowing why Ladoux pretended not to understand.

In Madrid, I wrote to Ladoux from my hotel. I asked him what was going on and why had the Brits taken me to Spain. I told him that I was anxiously awaiting further instructions from him—had he changed his mind and did he have new plans for me to try and extract information from a German in Spain, rather than a German in Belgium? I also asked him to send some more money, as my funds were getting rather low.

There was nothing for me to do in my hotel room, so after I wrote to Ladoux I went outside and took a walk. I walked into a fortune-teller's shop. Small yellow canaries and red finches were kept in cages all over the shop. They twittered and flew from the bars of their cage back to their swinging perches hanging from the center of their cages. The fortune-teller laid out her cards on a table, where the oil from the base of her palm had stained the wood dark from her holding the stack in her hand as her other hand did the work of flipping and placing the cards. The fortune-teller did just that in front of me. She flipped and placed, flipped and placed her cards. Will I be successful in my mission, will I receive the 1 million in francs? I asked the cards. Will I marry? Will Non finally come and live with me? The birds in their cages knew to be still while a fortune was read, and they watched the fortune-teller at work. Then the fortune-teller finally shook her head.

No, she said. You will be shot before any of that could possibly happen.

A bird then suddenly jumped from his perch to the side of the cage, and as he clung there, a shred of newspaper that had lined the tray beneath him now hung from his claw like a flag and fluttered in a breeze that went through the room.

Shot? I said.

The session is over, I've told you all the cards know, she said.

I paid with a ring from my finger. Van der Capellen had once given it to me. The stone set in the middle was made of cut glass, but the band was gold.

When I went through the glass-beaded curtain that hung in the doorway, it reflected light from the sun on the floor in the shapes of thousands of cut diamonds, and only if they were real, I thought, would I then fall to the floor on my knees, turning my skirt into a bowl to grab fistfuls of the diamonds and haul them away? Had the fortune-teller thought the same thing many a time before as she too sat staring at the sparkling diamond shapes on her well-worn floor? I turned back to look at the fortune-teller, but she was gone. She had disappeared into another room of her shop and all that was left were the birds, chirping loudly, as if trying to call her back.

In the dining room of the hotel a French colonel named Danvignes came up to me with a carnation he had plucked from the flower vase at the front desk and he tucked it into the bosom of my dress while he introduced himself. He then asked if he could share my table with me. I learned that in a few days he would be going back to France.

France? I said. You must do me a favor, I said.

Anything, he said, reaching out then to rearrange the carnation in my bosom, saying he didn't want it falling down beneath my neckline where no one could see it.

I am penniless, I explained. Please contact Captain Ladoux

and tell him to send me word, what am I to do next? Tell him I need money too, I said. That is very important. He sent me here to Spain, but meanwhile I have no money to pay even the hotel bill, and I'm spending my days doing nothing, waiting for his orders.

Colonel Danvignes then raised my fingers to his lips and kissed them. I will do it, he said, if you promise to see me again.

Yes, of course, I said. Let's have dinner together again before you leave.

Then I left the dining room. I had an idea. I went to the desk of the hotel porter. There, lying on the desk, was the diplomatic yearbook. I turned to the page of the German embassy. In town there was a German named Major Von Kalle. I decided to pay him a visit. While I was waiting in Madrid for word from Ladoux, I might as well spend my time wisely. What if Von Kalle could tell me some useful information about what the Germans were planning? Wouldn't that be worth the million francs Ladoux said he might pay me?

I knew just the right height to lift my dress above my ankles as I sat in a chair in Von Kalle's apartment. Von Kalle was curious as to why I had come to visit him, but I told him who I was and he had heard of me and my dancing career and he was pleased to have the company of an erudite woman and that was not something this war let him experience very often. His face was deeply scarred by adolescent acne, but his hair was thick and smooth and its beauty seemed to contrast sharply with his pitted skin, so that it almost seemed as if he were wearing a wig, but when he took me in his arms and started kissing me and I reached my fingers up toward his hair I found out that this of course was not true. Afterward he told me that he was tired, not from our lovemaking, but he had been busy with the preparation for a landing of German and Turkish soldiers from a submarine off the coast of Morocco, in the French zone.

It takes all my time, he said.

I told him that I hoped I did not tire him out too much, and he said that in fact I had injected new life into him, and then he asked where I was staying and I told him the Hotel Savoy.

But for how long, I don't know, I've run out of money, I said, and he then pulled 3,500 pesetas from his billfold and gave them to me.

Then he brushed back a smooth lock of hair that had fallen across the pock-riddled bridge of his nose and said that I should be a good girl and run along and I was treated to a fun slap on the rear and a tweak on the cheek as I was escorted out the front door.

A fine rain fell as I walked back to the Hotel Savoy, and it was so fine it felt more like a mist, and it hung in the air instead of falling, and I thought for a moment that I was back in Java, back in the forest, and that any moment I could look up and see a gibbon in a tree, but when I looked up from the ground all that I saw were men in a bar playing dominoes who, when I passed by, raised their glasses to their lips and stared at me through their pale amber beer.

Back at the hotel, Danvignes was sitting in the lobby, and when he saw me he rose from the chair with another carnation between his fingers. He was intent on placing it between my breasts again, but I took the carnation from him and told him to sit back down. I told him all about Von Kalle and about the German submarines landing in Morocco.

This is great news, woman! he said. You've done some fine intelligence work for your first time. But where, exactly, are the soldiers going to disembark? he said.

I don't know, I didn't want to seem overly curious, so I didn't ask him, I said.

But you must go back and find out! Danvignes said. You must go back right away. I'm leaving on a train tomorrow afternoon for Paris, and if I had that information it would be so useful, I could arrive at the Gare du Nord and take a taxi straight to Ladoux and tell him about the marvelous work you've done.

It was still raining the next morning when I walked down the street.

When I arrived at Von Kalle's, my skirts were almost completely soaked through with the persistent rain and I knew that the stray strands of hair by my temples had curled in the humidity into tight long ringlets like those worn by a Hasidic Jew.

Von Kalle did not open the door for me.

Enter, he said from inside his apartment after I had knocked. I entered, and his back was to me, and all I could see in the weak light was his smooth hair.

It's me, Mata Hari, I said. He still did not turn around, and then I realized that I did not want him to turn around. I did not want to see his scarred face, and maybe he knew this, and maybe that's why he had not turned around yet.

The French are sending radio messages all over, my dear, he said, inquiring about the German landings in Morocco. I wonder where they could have found that piece of information, he said.

Anyone could have obtained that information, I said. It wasn't me, if that's what you're suggesting, I said.

Then he turned and looked at me, and the wide, gaping craters, the acne scars by the sides of his mouth, elongated, changing into slits looking like the pupils in the eyes of a cobra, as he said to me, We have their code. We know it was you.

THE MISTAKE
OF THE MANICURIST

I HAD a picture of Non that I held in my hand as the train sped past Spaniards standing on ladders picking olives from the olive trees. I passed my hand over her hair in the picture. I touched my finger to the line of her jaw and remembered how it really was when she was a girl and how it felt with her small pulse beating under there and with the vibration of her throat as she spoke, the thrum of Mommy being said to me. With the train's wheels rolling on the tracks, I could feel that vibration again and I was with her on that train ride. I would have her back again someday, I thought, I would have Vadime as my husband and her as my child again and all that I needed to set the wheels in motion was the money Ladoux had promised me, and then I turned to look out at the Spaniards in the high, hot sun who wore their shirts tied by the sleeves around their foreheads and let their backs take the brunt of the burning rays and turn brown, but it was their heads they wanted shielded, I thought, so they would not get dizzy and could still work and get the job done. I was to remember those Spaniards in Paris while I walked to Ladoux's office and his secretary told me he was not there. I wanted the money Ladoux had promised for my intelligence work, but like the Spaniards who exposed their backs to save their heads from the burning sun, I too was exposing my back. Maybe it would have been better if I had never tried to see Ladoux again. Maybe he would have forgotten about me and let me go.

In Spain, before I left for France, I had asked Anna Lintjens to ask Van der Capellen to wire me money to the Banq Nacional de Paris. I needed money, any kind of money. I walked the streets waiting for the money to arrive.

I visited jewelry shops and tried on rings I would never own and that at times did not slide easily on my finger and that I could not even slide past my first digit and I had trouble pulling them off, and then I panicked, wondering if the rings were really on for good and how would I pay for them?

I read the newspaper. Germany launched an unrestricted warfare campaign. A German sub sank a French battleship. There were no survivors. General Joseph Joffre resigned as French commander in chief.

I went to have my nails done, and I asked the Asian girl with the fingers as long and thin as reeds and the hair as straight as chopsticks covering her eyes if she thought the Allies had a chance. I've been reading the newspaper, I told her, and I think the French have plenty to worry about, what with all the changes of command and the attacks. Then I looked across and saw a British soldier having his nails done by another Asian, and he was very relaxed, sitting in his salon chair, smoking a pipe and splaying out his pale, veiny hand across the Asian's counter. Out loud I wondered if the British would ever leave France, they would occupy France forever, I said, they like it here too much. Afterward, I did not like my nails painted dragon red, and I asked her to do them again, I asked her to do them French, and then I looked out the window while she set to doing them again and I looked at the men who had been following me for days now and I waved to them.

Finally, the money from Van der Capellen arrived at the Banq Nacional de Paris.

I wrote to Vadime, I told him how I was trying hard to earn money so that we could finally start our life together. I told him all about Non in the letter. I told him how as a baby she would curl in my lap and poke the stems of flowers through my long braids and how I was sure he would like her, because I had been told she was like me. I was writing all this when there was no knock at the door, just the feel of the wind rushing through as the door opened quickly, and then the quick spread of warmth I could feel from the five policemen who stood there, taking up all the space there was in the small room I rented and sweating under their hats while they told me I was under arrest. When I told them it must be a mistake, that Captain Ladoux should be notified and that he'd clear it all up, they showed me the arrest notice and at the bottom it was signed by Ladoux, in his cramped hand with the last letter sitting almost upright, looking more like a cross than an X, and I thought, He probably signs his name like that on purpose, so people will think he is closer to God than the rest of us.

Later, in my cell, I looked down at my fingers and noticed how the Asian manicurist had left some lacquer. I could see the faint lines of the dragon red beneath the cuticles, which should have been a pinkish cream, in the French style, and not this seeping in of red, a hint of pouring blood.

SOME CHEEK

GET UP FROM THE FLOOR, Mata Hari said to Sister Leonide. Stop your praying. The floor is filthy. You'll spoil your habit. But Sister Leonide would not get up, and so while Sister Leonide was still on the floor Mata Hari knelt beside her and she lifted the black cloth of Sister Leonide's habit and she held the cloth between the knuckles of both her fists and she rubbed. Sister Leonide reached out and grabbed Mata Hari's hands in her own and she turned to her.

Pray with me, she said. Mata Hari looked down at Sister Leonide's hands. They were dry and rough.

You need cream, Mata Hari said. Sister Leonide then smoothed back the hair from Mata Hari's face and a tear fell from Mata Hari's eye and Sister Leonide wiped it away and Mata Hari stood slowly, her knees hurting her, and she said, I don't know how you nuns do it all day.

AT TRIAL, Adolphe Messimy, the ministry of war, wasn't present to testify in Mata Hari's defense. A letter was read out loud, written by his wife.

I'm sorry to inform you that my husband's bout with rheumatism has prevented him from attending this trial. Besides, she wrote, *the whole thing must be a mistake, my husband says he's never even met the indicated person.*

Mata Hari laughed. He's got some cheek, she said, and her laughter was infectious and all the men laughed because Mata Hari had been Monseigneur Messimy's mistress off and on for a long time and he had been called as a witness for the defense because he could testify that she never, not once, while they were in each other's arms, or while he was entering her from behind (the way he preferred, à la chien, he had said), did she ever discuss the war and if she were really a spy, wouldn't the ministry of war be the best person to obtain information from while his genitals, dangling only by a thin wing of aged skin, were being caressed with her fingers whose nails were richly painted with a lacquer named Orient Plum Surprise?

Jules Cambon was then called to the stand. He swore that he and Mata Hari never spoke of the war or his work. What did you discuss then?, he was asked.

Ancient Rome, the pyramids, wine, and horse racing, he said. Mata Hari remembered that with the gentle Jules Cambon, ambassador in several military posts, there was more talk than anything else. Every time he tried to enter her, he was flaccid and he would spend countless minutes trying to stuff his penis inside of her, insisting that it would become hard once it was inside of her. That is when she would stroke his brow and bring up a topic like horse racing. He was very well versed in it and knew bloodlines back to Arabia, and simple things too, like pastes of cloves and garlic and witch hazel used for poultices to wrap up horses' swollen ankles. Out loud, in the dark, they weighed together the benefits of training horses on a hard track or a soft track, the use of a German martingale or just a standard martingale found hanging in almost every barn.

THE GAME

It was hot in the courtroom. She was sweating at the hairline beneath the blue three-cornered hat that she wore. They were all waiting for a thunderstorm to come, and men in the courtroom kept looking out the high windows to see if the rain had begun to fall. Except she wasn't trying to look out the windows, she was looking at the door. She was hoping to see Non walk through, under the bust of Marianne, symbol of the republic, even though she'd been told that Non hadn't been called as a witness. What used to be hanging above the door instead of the bust of Marianne was the figure of Christ on the cross. She wished it was still there. She would have preferred an image of his nailed palms and his bloody wrists and his halo of spiked thorns and his pathetic, thin white limbs, his legs crossed at the bony ankles to the image of Marianne and how she looked down upon her, because it was the same look Bouchardon wore when he looked at her, a woman he hated because she had taken advantage of men for her own gain and who he believed had endangered the lives of men who defended their country. She was incalculably worse than even the enemy was in the eyes of the wooden Marianne and the fingernail-biting Bouchardon and to how many more men in the courtroom at the time, she had no way of knowing.

She thought she may have had a chance at being set free, though. Wasn't it clear to some of these men as it was clear to her, she thought, that she was never really a spy for Germany?

She could hear the rumble of the thunder far off. It came from the direction of Rouen, from the north, where there were farmhouses and green fields and fields of corn, whose silk tips wavered in the wind while Vadime Masloff's deposition was read out loud. To quote, he said, that the affair I had with the accused meant little to me. He added that he was not aware, in any way whatsoever, that she had been employed into the services of either the French republic or any republic for that matter.

She thought what he wrote in his deposition was clever, the court would believe she was just a passing whim to him and there would be no reason to implicate him as well. There might still be a chance that they would be together after all.

The storm was getting closer. The bust of Marianne appeared even darker in the courtroom, she looked more like a ship's bowsprit then, her features weathered rough and menacing by wind and splashed dark with spray. When the storm finally did reach them, there was only a muffled boom of thunder and then a few glimpses that did not seem like bolts, but more like a weak glow of lantern lights seen flashing in some faraway field, nothing more than a farmer's nightly inspection of his budding crops and planted rows. The heat remained and left them in the same hot stupor as before, while the storm crawled its way toward the south.

IN THIS HEAT

IT WAS in this heat that the seven jurors, members of the third Permanent Council of War of the Military Government of Paris, all arrived at their verdict. Mata Hari sat next to her lawyer, Clunet, in the courtroom, and every once in a while he took her hand. His own hand was moist with sweat and she wished he wouldn't hold it, especially after she noticed how yellow and ridged his nails had become with age, and that was a detail she hadn't noticed in the poor light of her prison cell these past few months, but then she thought he needed someone to hold onto more than she did. After all, she had walked across the sea once as a girl and she believed she could do it again, only this time the sea wasn't sand and salt but a roomful of old men she had to wade through, their spectacles sitting on the bridges of their noses, their graying hair matted with sweat dropping at their temples, their cheeks starred, asterisked with the small broken lines of blood vessels, and their eyes dull with passing clouds seen in them, the weather of the old. She let Clunet take her hand, poor man, he is no different from one of these old men, and together they listened to the verdict.

She was told to rise from her chair. When she stood she straightened her coat and made sure her skirt hung properly around her and was not clinging to her because of the sweat that she could feel dribbling down the backs of her knees and the lengths of her muscled calves.

In the name of the Republic of France, we find the defendant guilty.

Clunet grabbed onto her as if to shield her from the words being read aloud. She wanted to speak. She said something, but Clunet could not hear her. His hearing was not what it used to be, and the men in the room were all murmuring to one another. Ma petite, ma petite, he said loudly as if it were she who had trouble hearing instead. Later, when leaving the courtroom he was asked by others what she had said to him, and he replied, She said, It's impossible. Impossible.

THROUGH BIRDS OF PARADISE

I DID NOT SAY Impossible. I said, I know now what she saw. At the exact moment that I was in the courtroom and was pronounced guilty, I remembered an incident that I had put out of my mind the moment it had happened years and years ago. If you had asked me before if I had ever believed that a memory like that could be so instantaneously wiped clean, I would have laughed, I would have asked what you'd been drinking, I would have joked, Have you any left? Then pour me some, I would have said.

When I was pronounced guilty I forgot where I was, and I was thrown back in time into the heat of Java, and what I was condemned for was not being some absurd German spy with letters and numbers for a name. I was guilty of something much worse.

It was a hot night, and MacLeod wasn't there. If you had asked me then, I might have lied for him, I might have said he was out with the other officers, a late-night meeting over dinner and billiards and the passing of tightly wrapped cigars, when really there was no other place he was except with a girl, a teenager most likely who did as she was told in a velvet-wallpapered room in the gabled whorehouse in town.

I had just checked on Non and Norman, and they were sleeping together as they sometimes liked to, their heads turned toward each other with their hairlines almost touching, like lovers discussing secrets in the dark. I shut the door and left the room and went out to the garden where it was cooler. Tekul was there. He never wore a shirt and his brown back looked almost gray in the moonlight, like cool stone. Where's Kidul? I asked, and he nodded in the direction of their bedroom where she was sleeping. He was smoking a cigarette, and he asked me to sit down with him on a reed mat he had laid on the grass. I had never known Tekul ever to sit in a chair. He patted the mat with his hand, saying it was cooler closer to the earth. Come see, he said, and so I did, and he was right, and through my sarong I could feel the coolness creeping up into me.

Master not home tonight? he said. I did not have to nod. Tekul nodded for me. We both knew where MacLeod was. I think I sighed, though, and Tekul passed me his cigarette and I smoked it.

Good, no? he said, and that is when I tasted the cigarette in my mouth and realized it was not tobacco, but he was right, it tasted good, as if vanilla had been added to it.

Tekul, what is this? I asked.

Island secret, he said, smiling.

It did not take long before the cigarette started to take effect. I thought there was a movement behind the birds of paradise. I thought I saw them part and I thought I saw the smallest of hands clutching on the stems, pulling them aside.

Look, don't you see? I said to Tekul. Then he took my hand.

Nothing there, just inside your mind, he said. You have to do this right, ma'am, he said. You have to not worry. You worry, you will have a bad time with the power of the island secret.

Mengerti? he said, and then he said, Come, lie down, and he took me and had me lie back on the cool reed mat and he looked down at me.

In the dark, I could see the whites of his eyes and they shone wetly, forming perfect rings around his pupils. They looked like the white rings on the side of ships that were thrown to rescue people who had fallen overboard. I kept looking at them, telling myself they could save my life. Then I felt Tekul's fingers on me. He reached up into my sarong and slid his hand on my leg above my knee and touched me as gently as if he were a breeze, and I felt myself feeling the warmth of his hand and his fingertips and being amazed that I enjoyed the warmth, when for so long I had been complaining of the heat of the island. Soon I felt his face upon my shirt. He moved the cloth aside with his teeth and put his mouth on my breast. Meanwhile, his hand did not stop, it reached farther up into me and found me wet. Tekul, this is not right, I said, and I tried to push him away, but Tekul gently laughed and from his laugh I could smell the smoke from his cigarette and then I could taste it because my mouth was open while he laughed, and at the same time I tasted it, he entered me, and I did not know how much I wanted to feel him inside me until he was there, pushing into me. In a climax that seemed to have a flight pattern, where I flew over hills and mountains, then down below the mantle of the earth, I floated through slow-moving magma, then up again I sprang from a desert, shedding the sand like water droplets as I headed straight up and then across, seeing hundreds of pink and red sunrises and sunsets, a speeded-up lifetime of many souls, and then I landed in a talking river where branches splashed in a rushing current and pebbles rolled, their knocking sound a gentle conversation, a hush to be quiet from a mother to her child, and then awash, onshore, newly come to life, I opened my eyes while on the reed mat, still in my garden.

You've done well, Tekul said, and that is when I turned and looked and saw Non. It was really her behind the birds of paradise, her hands I saw, not some hands I had imagined while in a hazy drugged state.

Her mouth was shut tight, her lips one line, and I thought for a moment that she had been through my cosmetics, had found my lip paint and had drawn the line herself, some girlish play I had not yet known she was ready for. But it was not lip paint. It was the look of a girl who has seen her mother naked and the servant's body, not her father's body, moving in her mother and over her, the bodies stuck so close together they may have well been a flat rock stuck in mud, and unstuck what would crawl out but mandibled, pincered, million-legged things, their tails in scythelike curves.

I pushed Tekul off me. He was so light, no thicker than a cattail and almost the same brown, that I could fling him, really, and he landed in the tangled vines where house cats kept by long-ago renters of our house now lived wild and defecated through the leaves. There was no consoling her. She ran from me. Since when had she become so fast? Or was I so slow? Was the cigarette Tekul had given me still at work? I could barely move. I heard her slam the bedroom door. I looked up to the window of her bedroom, but it was not she who was standing behind the curtain, but Kidul, her horror something she clenched in her fists at her chest. I noticed the curtain blowing from side to side in front of her, as if it were a cloth working to erase a classroom's chalked letters from the slate.

I do not remember all the rest. Maybe I tried to console them both. Maybe I explained to Kidul how the drug had turned me into someone else. Maybe I pleaded with her to understand that what her husband meant to me was nothing at all. Maybe I tried to pull Non from her hiding place behind the bamboo chair and tell her what she saw was just a play. We had been actors. We had parts. I was the evil princess and Tekul the kris-dagger god come to slay me. Maybe I put both Norman and Non back to bed. I brought them rice milk from the kitchen served in wineglasses. Let's be elegant, I might have said. Let's pretend we are in the house of the king and the queen, I said, and tied my hair behind my head because when it was loose and falling by my face I had noticed it still held the smell of Tekul's secret island cigarette.

Then, only days later, when the children were poisoned and it was Kidul who had done it, the memory of the night with Tekul was gone from my thoughts. I blamed MacLeod instead.

What Non remembered of that night with me I have no way of knowing. She never mentioned anything to me about it, but now, looking back at it while in my cell after the trial, I realized that throughout the years, it was not just MacLeod who kept Non from seeing me, it was probably Non herself. She hated me for having hurt Kidul, who was her loving nanny, her playmate, and the one who bathed her from a brown ceramic pitcher whose stream of water she held above her head, telling her stories of the mountain gods while she rinsed her hair of ginger soap and later scented it with myrrh. And she hated me because it was my fault her brother was dead.

How stupid of me, I thought, and I pounded my leg with my fist in disgust and anger, and Sister Leonide, who was in the cell with me, caught my fist in midair and held it, bringing the back of my hand close to her mouth, where she kissed it. Then she told me to have faith and to have courage, maybe there could be a retrial. I looked at her for a moment, thinking of a way she might be right, that Non could see it all a different way, but then I realized Sister Leonide was talking about the trial in which I was condemned for being a spy.

Oh, the trial, I said. That is what you mean. Sentenced to death, I said. I could not think about it now. Of course, I said. A just punishment. And I thought how I wished it was the next morning that I would be shot, because I did not think I could live another day knowing that it was my fault that my Non and Norm had been taken from me. I looked at my prison wall, but I did not study its stone surface. Instead I saw Non again, refusing to let me kiss her good-night while she lay in bed next to Norm, how she turned away from me and buried her head in the pillow and hunched her back so her shoulders stuck up sharply like axe blades hidden in her gown. All that I could kiss of her was her thick, dark hair, smelling of Kidul's myrrh.

AN INQUIRY
ABOUT THE GARDEN

DR. BIZARD WAS in his garden with a watering can, watering his radishes, when he received a phone call from the prison and heard the news. He had hoped that the thunderstorm would have done the job for him, and he had turned and scowled at the passing clouds when they did not produce any rain, only a dark green sky that made his radishes appear less red and almost sickly in the light.

When he arrived at the prison, he expected her to be crying into her pillow on the bed. He had brought a calmative too, just in case. When he got there, it was not she who was lying down and crying, but Sister Leonide. Dr. Bizard looked at Mata Hari and noticed for the first time how she looked like all the other prisoners in the building. She no longer looked as if she were lengthening, and her squat neck seemed to sit deep within her collarbone. Her fingers did not seem all that long, but fatter now at the knuckles and arthritic in their appearance. She did not look as if her entire body was striving to be set free. She was rubbing her hand on Sister Leonide's back, comforting her, bending close to her ear. When Mata Hari saw Dr. Bizard, she said, Finally, you're here, and she held out her hand to Dr.

Bizard to take the calmative from him so she could give it to Sister Leonide. When Sister Leonide sat up, one could see how she was clasping her silver cross while she lay on the bed and now on her cheek there was an imprint of the cross, where it had dug into her skin.

The knees of Dr. Bizard's pants were brown with dirt.

How is your garden? Mata Hari asked. And Dr. Bizard remembered that is how some of his other patients who were told they would be shot would talk to him after they had learned the news. How they talked as if nothing had changed at all. They were most normal then, he thought, and he remembered some patients who beforehand had been so lunatic he could not have received a reply from them that made any sense, but once they were sentenced, it was as if a great calm had fallen onto them and they spoke in clear, full sentences, their eyes looked directly at him, and they looked more like leaders then, great rulers or presidents, people you would entrust to make life-changing decisions, and they did not bear any resemblance to the thieves and murderers they were when they first came.

A shame about the rain, Mata Hari said, I bet your vegetables could have used a good watering.

I've heard the news, Dr. Bizard said. I'm sorry.

How does it happen? Do they all aim for the heart? Or is it the head?

After she said this, Sister Leonide sobbed loudly, and Dr. Bizard passed her his handkerchief.

I don't know what they'll do this time, Dr. Bizard said. I can inquire if you wish.

By now, Sister Leonide had taken to crying steadily again and

Mata Hari leaned over her and put her arm around her. Through her crying, Sister Leonide said, I should be the one consoling you, I should be praying for you.

Don't worry, Mata Hari said. You were never a good nun anyway. You were probably a better cleaning lady. You were probably the best in all of France.

ANOTHER PLAN

VAN DER CAPELLEN missed Mata Hari. She had been gone so long from Holland that he was beginning to think she had left altogether and had moved back to France for good, though she had always assured him she would return soon. He wondered if she had found a new lover and he looked in the mirror and could not blame her if she had.

He had gained weight recently and it all had gone right to his middle so that when he looked down he could not see the tops of his shoes. His neck, also, had gained weight and his collars were so tight that his wife noticed and one morning she said it looked as if it hurt him just to swallow his coffee and she said she would have the tailor make him some new shirts that fit him, extralarge in the collar she said. Mata Hari, he thought, never would have said anything about his fat middle or neck, though, and she would have taken him in her arms and kissed him and made love to him and later that month he would remember, dutifully, to send money to her house, which he himself had made the down payment on.

He never would have gone directly to her house before. They would always meet in a hotel room, but he knew the address, of course, and one day he found himself walking down her street. He rang the bell and the maid answered the door.

Anna Lintjens invited Van der Capellen in and he sat on the sofa and she brought him tea and hoped that the legs of the sofa, now weak and in need of the screws being tightened or even replaced, would withstand the weight of his build.

Van der Capellen held his tea as if he were just about to take a sip of it for the longest time, but he didn't. Instead he spoke of Mata Hari. He spoke of how he missed her and he asked Anna Lintjens to forgive him for coming here and talking of it with her, but there was no one else, you see, he could talk to about it, and he was almost beginning to think that Mata Hari hadn't existed at all and that he had made her up.

Anna Lintjens assured him how real Mata Hari was and said she was also worried about the whereabouts of her employer. It had been weeks since she had heard from her and that was unusual. There was the house to look after. There was the leak in the roof that still needed patching. In the last rain the clothes in one of Mata Hari's closets and some of her most treasured silk sarongs had become soaked and their colors ran and bled together.

Van der Capellen told Anna Lintjens that he would pay for a roofer to come and nail shingles over the damaged section of roof and then he asked in a small voice, not looking Anna Lintjens in the eye, if she thought there was a possibility of another man in Mata Hari's life. Anna Lintjens immediately said no, that was out of the question, but of course she thought to herself how she had just told a lie, there was a young Russian named Vadime whom Mata Hari would soon marry.

You don't agree? Van der Capellen said when he saw Anna Lintjens shaking her head.

I'm sorry, would you repeat what you just said, Anna Lintjens said.

The consulate, Van der Capellen said, I think I should go there and make inquiries. I think they could file a report with the French consulate. There is a war going on, after all. What if she, I can't bear to think of it, but what if she's hurt? What if she's lying in the middle of some bombed-out building or alone in some hospital bed dazed and confused?

Yes, of course, you should go to the consulate. Go right away, Anna Lintjens said. She stood and took Van der Capellen's cup from him, even though he had not drunk one sip.

Just one thing, before I go, Van der Capellen said, I was wondering if maybe there was something of Mata Hari's that I could have. I know it's a silly question. I'm a silly man, perhaps. But it would help so much if I could just have something, anything really, even something she wore, it would help me get through the lonely periods. I think you understand, he said.

Anna Lintjens knew he would like her to reach into Mata Hari's top dresser drawer and produce for him one of her black satin panties, but of course she would not do it. Then she remembered, right beside her in the easy chair was her sewing box, it was filled with scraps of Mata Hari's old costumes, which Anna Lintjens had kept because she liked the colors or the beads that had been sewn into them. There was one section of cloth that was from the shoulder of a costume and it was sewn with a row of ruby red beads, and Anna held it up and gave it to Van der Capellen and told him that the cloth was from a section of cleavage of one of her costumes. There, that should be close enough to what he wanted, she thought, a piece of something that had rested on the warm skin of Mata Hari's breasts and Van der Capellen was happy to receive the stray bit of cloth and he wanted to kiss it the moment it touched his hands, but he didn't, of course, not in the presence of the maid, and instead he folded it carefully and put it into his pocket.

He fingered the ruby red beads while he waited in line to fill out forms in the consulate office and twiddled his fingertip across one bead over and over again and imagined it being her nipple and he hoped when the woman behind the desk was ready to wait on him that the throbbing erection he had would have gone down and he tried not to touch the bead for a moment, but he couldn't help himself, and by the time he reached the consulate woman's desk and sat down in the chair that she offered him, he was sure, although he could not see for himself because of the size of his belly, that his fly was sticking straight up like a tent pole and the cloth of his pants was the canvas that covered it.

The consulate woman had a nice smile. It wasn't altogether straight and one side of her lips reached up higher on her face than the other, and it made her seem as if she weren't quite sure of herself, which Van der Capellen found attractive and different, very different from Mata Hari, whose dark, almost Asian eyes and perfectly straight lips never hinted at any type of wavering stance whatsoever and always seemed to him to mean she knew exactly what she was doing and why.

So it wasn't a surprise to him, really, thinking back on it, that after he learned through a series of weeks passing that Mata Hari was being held in a prison for some kind of espionage act that he asked the consulate woman out to dinner and later to a hotel and that he no longer carried the cloth with the ruby red beads in his pocket but had left it in some drawer at his office, along with some broken-nibbed pens and a small assortment of corks to bottles of wines he once had at lunch and liked and kept because he thought he might try them one day again but never did.

Anna Lintjens read the letter he wrote telling her that he had found the whereabouts of Mata Hari, that she was in Saint-Lazare, accused of espionage, that he would no longer be sending a monthly check and that he thought Anna Lintjens might understand.

Accused of espionage! Anna Lintjens thought, and she felt as if she could hit herself for not having come out of her room that night that she heard the sneaky Kramer come to the door with his vials of invisible ink tinkling against one another in Mata Hari's hands as she took them. How she wished she had burst out of her room at the time of the knock at the door and told Kramer to leave and let her employer be.

What did her employer know of vials of secret ink? What did she know of codes and code names? Her employer was a dancer, why was he giving her the name H21?

Anna Lintjens sank back into her chair and let Van der Capellen's letter fall from her fingertips and onto the floor she had just waxed and polished. There was no way she could think of to save her employer now. What could she do? Scale a prison wall? Bake a cake concealed with a saw-bladed knife? Bribe a guard? And with what money? she said to herself. Then she rose from her chair, picked up the letter, threw it away, and headed to her room. From her dresser drawer, wrapped in a holey silk stock-

THE PIRATE

Dr. VanVoort had a servant living with him who was as brown as one of the coffee beans on his plantation. Her Dutch was not good, so she tried to teach him Malay. He knew how to say things like *spoon* and *good* and *night* and *shelf,* but he did not know enough words to carry on a conversation with the girl, say about politics, but then of course there were no politics to discuss on the plantation, unless you counted the division of labor, who would be the workers today to harvest the beans, who would be the ones to grind them?

She seemed to be the opposite of Mata Hari physically. When she lay down naked on the bed for him each night, she had no visible third eye between her legs. It was there, he knew, but its positioning was more posterior and did not look out at anything except the darkness that her own closed legs created. He wondered if Mata Hari had ever made it to Paris. He wondered what she was doing now. Was she in the drawing room of some ambassador, were they discussing the latest events of the war?

Some days he dreamed of leaving and trying to find her there, but he was not certain where to look and then he would catch sight of himself in a mirror. His hair was thinning and his scalp showed through red all the time from too much sun so he had taken to wearing a cloth over his head and he looked to himself more like a pirate than a physician and he thought how Mata Hari would probably not even recognize him now.

His brown servant girl called to him that dinner was ready and he sat the way she did, cross-legged on a straw mat, and the tables in the house were all piled high with old newspapers he had read over and over again and would still read, taking one with him after his morning coffee and heading toward the outhouse made of thin bamboo poles that let decent-size bars of sunlight through to read by, and that in the strong winds that sometimes swept through would topple over and he'd have to right the outhouse, and he and his servant would inspect the damage to the ties that held the poles together, and then they would work side by side, nimble fingers at repair.

SHE IS

ANNA LINTJENS went and pawned the emerald ring. The dealer held his eyepiece so long to his eye and fingered the ring in his hand, looking at it so long that Anna Lintjens was beginning to worry that it was fake. Finally, he put down his eyepiece and handed Anna Lintjens more money than she had ever held in her hand at one time. The small purse she had strung to the waist of her dress was not large enough for the roll of guilders so at first she carried them, but then she feared a robber might catch sight of her holding them so she turned into a doorway and stuffed them down into one cup of her brassiere.

While preparing for her journey, packing dresses and petticoats into a trunk, there was a knock at the door. She went to the window and looked down at the stoop and there was Non, her wavy black hair spread over her shoulders and holding a satchel of books and a Mata Hari biscuit tin.

The biscuit tin's thin layer of paint was fading and the silver of the metal was showing through beneath the painted hair of Mata Hari and her hair looked more silver than brown. Anna Lintjens invited her in, and Non, who had never been in her mother's house, walked up to the paintings on the walls of the living room and touched their frames and she touched the back of the sofa and she even touched the handle of the fireplace poker.

Anna Lintjens asked if her father knew she had come here, and Non answered that her father didn't live in The Hague any longer and that no, her aunt Louise didn't know she had decided to come and finally visit her mother.

Anna Lintjens took the girl upstairs and showed her Mata Hari's room and she pulled out Mata Hari's album and Non took it to the bed and together they sat and looked through it and Non kept saying how beautiful her mother had been and Anna Lintjens would correct her verb tense, saying, Is, how beautiful she is.

Anna Lintjens took down some of Mata Hari's costumes from her closet and laid them on the bed to show Non, and Non asked if Anna Lintjens thought it would be all right if she tried on one of the costumes, if she thought that her mother would mind, and Anna Lintjens was sure Mata Hari wouldn't mind, and she left the girl alone for a while, for a long time actually, because Anna Lintjens had fallen asleep in the chair in the living room and when she woke she looked at the clock and realized she would never have time to call for a cab and catch that day's train headed to Paris so she would have to wait until the next day. She went and peeked through a crack in Mata Hari's door. Non was wearing one of Mata Hari's gold breastplates and her silk skirts and a veil over her head and she was dancing around the room and singing a song in a language Anna Lintjens didn't know but she guessed must have been Malay and she watched for a while.

The dancing was beautiful, and even though Anna Lintjens had never seen Mata Hari dance a performance, she felt she could say that now she had, because she imagined it to be as beautiful a dance as her daughter, Non, had danced.

Before Non left, Anna Lintjens gave Non a gift. She dug through Mata Hari's huge jewelry box and found a gold-plated watch and put it on Non's wrist and said she knew that Mata Hari would want her to have it. You'll have to take it off when you see your aunt Louise, of course, Anna Lintjens warned her, or else she'll take it from you and make sure you never come here again.

Can I come again? asked Non. And Anna Lintjens answered yes by giving the girl a kiss on the cheek and smelling at the same time the fragrance of mimosa that the girl must have taken off Mata Hari's shelf and dabbed behind her ears.

I hope that next time I come, my mother is here, Non said, and Anna Lintjens said, I hope so too, and she was about to close the door on the girl when Non turned around and looked at Anna Lintjen's head, and said, You've got pins in your bun, you know.

Ah, so I have, Anna Lintjens said, and pushed them deeper down into her hair bun so that they could not be seen.

IN A CLOUD

VADIME MASLOFF PLAYED a harmonica in the trench, but he wasn't very good at it, and another soldier grabbed it from him and threw it up and out of the trench, where he could hear it being shot at. He hadn't lost sight in both his eyes and in fact had regained his sight in the eye that had originally been damaged by the shelling and he was back in the trench again, cuddling with the rats at night and staring up at the sky in the day, reading shapes into clouds, swearing to himself that he saw Mata Hari floating by, her arms cumulus striations, spread out as if to embrace him.

He did not believe she had been spying, and when he received the letters warning him not to have relations with her, asking him for a deposition, he did what he thought was best and wrote that the relationship meant very little to him. He hoped that they wouldn't arrest him and think he was a spy too, because he wanted to be there when Mata Hari was set free.

He would wait for her forever, he thought while he took off his wool papakha from his head and examined it, seeing how it was balding in places, the rats at night in his sleep biting out bits of it, thinking its warm fibers ideal for building a nest for their young. He sighed, he tried fishing for his harmonica by tying a string to the carved handle of his sharp-bladed bebout and dragging it across the surface of the ground up above.

What he dragged into the trench was dirt, a dud of a stick grenade, and a few good-size field rocks that fell on his head, but no harmonica. Damn you, Ivan, he said to the other soldier, who had thrown his harmonica out and who was now lying on his back, watching the clouds. Vadime squatted next to Ivan and pointed to the cloud with the arms held out for an embrace and said up there was his girlfriend, his wife-to-be, and Ivan said, Don't be ridiculous, that's my mother and sister up there throwing me down kisses.

NEVER SURE

THE JOURNEY FROM Holland to France, Anna Lintjens thought, was taking longer than she thought it would, even though the train sped past scenery so quickly she was not sure what she saw. Was it trees? Was it houses? A field of cows? If one can never be sure of what one sees when traveling, she thought to herself, then what is the point of the journey?

BLANKETS

IT WAS a cold morning and Mata Hari slept with her head under the covers, breathing her own exhaled air just to keep warm. The cold was again fingering its way through the spaces between the stones of the wall of her cell.

Sister Leonide came as usual with her cup of coffee, and Mata Hari sat on her cot with her wool blanket draped over her shoulders while she drank it.

Mata Hari's reflection in the coffee made her face look swollen and she told Sister Leonide that the kitchen was really getting worse, that it wasn't serving coffee that was coffee any longer, but something with brown grease, leavings from something fried in a pan, scraped into hot water, and stirred quite possibly, she said. The kitchen can kill you, did you know that? Mata Hari said, and Sister Leonide nodded, even though she did not know what Mata Hari was talking about, but she thought it best not to disagree with Mata Hari and to try and be as understanding as possible, because Mata Hari, who did not know it, would be shot the next morning.

But this is still probably better than what poor Vadime is drinking in the trenches, Mata Hari said, and then Sister Leonide nodded and thought to remind herself after the lights went out that night to cover the corridors leading to the cells with blankets so the sound of the men who came to take the prisoner to the firing squad stomping through in their shiny black shoes would not be so loud. Sister Leonide knew the men would come through as noisily as possible, so the prisoner would already be awake when they arrived at the prisoner's cell, and she always thought how rude it was to startle a fast-asleep prisoner that way in the predawn hours when she did not know that today was the day she would die.

That was the law, not to let a prisoner know the date of his or her execution. Sister Leonide wasn't sure why, maybe because it made the prisoner easier to handle and take out of the cell if she was taken by surprise or maybe it was because it was considered cruel to live out your last days knowing you had an appointment with death.

THE DOUBLE DOSE

OUTSIDE, A FRONT had come through and the air was heavy with mist and it amplified the sounds inside the prison.

She told Sister Leonide she thought she could hear Charles, the guard, swallowing at the end of the corridor. She thought she could also hear the voices of other women in the prison. Was a prostitute crying? A baby killer laughing? An adulteress singing? A spy screaming? She closed her eyes and spoke. Let me tell you about the day I walked across the sea to Ameland and back. I felt the small sand crabs beneath my bare feet. I waved to the seals sunning themselves on sand flats. The hen pen and gutweed clung to my ankles. A black-headed gull flew in one direction, while in another direction flew a barnacle goose, sounding out his call. I turned and looked behind me and there was the great gray wall of the tide and I realized for the first time that it looked more like a rain-filled cloud rolling in close to the ground. Then she opened her eyes and grabbed Sister Leonide's hands, and she said, Maybe, just maybe, it wasn't the tide coming in after all and that I have been wrong all these years. Maybe it was just a cloud, and like a cloud encountered on the trail of a high mountaintop, a person can pass through it and come out the other side, still standing, still alive.

Later Dr. Bizard came by to see how she was doing.

I haven't seen you for a while, doctor, she said. To what do I owe the pleasure?

He shrugged his shoulders and the sound receiver of his stethoscope reflected the light from the gas lamp onto the floor and then onto the wall and then onto the floor again.

I've got something for you, he said. But, shh, keep it quiet. From one trouser pocket he pulled a leather-covered flask. From his other pocket he pulled out his handkerchief, and wrapped inside were two shot glasses.

He had been working in the garden again, and the nails of his fingers were packed with soil as he poured the drinks, saying it was Russian vodka. When she took the shot glass from him, she wrapped her hand around his and brought his hand to her nose, saying it had been too long since she had smelled the earth.

SISTER LEONIDE was waiting for Dr. Bizard to leave Mata Hari's cell. When she saw him walk down the corridor past the guard's desk, she asked if Mata Hari was asleep yet. She knew he had been planning to give her a double dose of chloral that night, so that her last night of sleep would be a good one.

She's sound asleep, he said to Sister Leonide, and so Sister Leonide began to spread the wool blankets in the corridor leading to Mata Hari's cell and even before she was finished laying all the blankets, curious rats had come out and the breeze created by the blankets floating up in the air and then coming down on the stone floor made the rats shut their eyes, and lay back their ears, in anticipation for whatever blow might come their way.

A NECESSARY BREEZE

Again, the money Anna Lintjens held in her hand was a thick wad of bills, but this time in francs, not guilders, and again she put the money into the cup of her brassiere, where, when the horse-drawn cab trotted on the cobblestones, the bills rubbed back and forth on her breast. She was hot, even though it was a cold morning, and she wondered if when she presented her roll of francs to the guard the roll would be wet with her sweat and would that sour the plan? She lifted the neckline of her dress up and down a few times, trying to send a breeze through to keep the bills dry.

THE DAY OF EXPIATION

CHARLES DIDN'T LIKE the size of his Adam's apple. It made it difficult to shave and often the blade nicked him, as it did the morning Mata Hari's execution was scheduled. He was holding a handkerchief to the bleeding cut throughout his morning coffee, and even after he had dressed in his uniform and sat at his post in the corridor, he still held the handkerchief close to his Adam's apple and wondered if the bleeding would stop by the time Bouchardon and his men came to get the prisoner. It didn't.

The men came and said good morning to him, and while he led the way with his keys hanging from his belt he still held the handkerchief to his Adam's apple, and he cursed the nun, because walking on the woolen blankets was slippery and he was not sure of his footing and would have liked to have been able, in case he fell, to have both hands free and not one occupied with a cut on his throat.

Ahead of them went another guard, who, with a long wax taper, lit the gas lamps that lined the corridor and when he did, the rats, sleeping under the blankets, scurried off, their forms seen under the wool, just small, dark, moving humps one had to be careful not to trip over.

Mata Hari was sound asleep. She did not hear the men coming. The double dose of chloral that Dr. Bizard had given her was very effective. It was Sister Leonide who had to shake her awake. When she sat up she saw Bouchardon and the men standing in her cell, and before she could say anything Bouchardon spoke.

Have courage, he said, the time for your expiation has come.

She leaned on the metal rail at the end of her cot and stood up. Sister Leonide hugged her and began to cry and Mata Hari made Sister Leonide step back so she could see her face and she held Sister Leonide's arms and said, Don't worry, Sister, I shall know how to die.

May I wear a corset? she asked Dr. Bizard, who was also in the room, and he nodded his head.

She began to get dressed. She put one foot on her thin mattress and began to roll her silk stockings up her ankles and her long dancer's legs. Sister Leonide didn't want the others to see her bare legs and so she stood between Mata Hari and the men and Mata Hari smiled and told Sister Leonide, Now is not the time to be prudish.

A trunk with the clothes that she had with her at the time of her arrest had been returned to her. From it she pulled out a pearl gray dress and a felt tricorn hat and shoes that buttoned up to her ankles.

When she was completely dressed she asked what the weather was like outside.

Charles answered her and said it was misty and cold and she nodded her head at that, and said, Good, it really will be like walking through a cloud then and she threw her blue wool coat over her shoulders like a cape.

Walking down the gaslit corridor, over the woolen blankets, Charles finally took away his handkerchief from his Adam's apple and put it in his pocket and went to take Mata Hari's arm, but she brushed him away and instead she took the arm of Sister Leonide.

Downstairs, before they left the building and the bolt was lifted to the door of the prison, she asked for a pen and some paper.

She wrote to Non.

Dear Non,

I have never told you the story of the woman who cheated death. It is a good story, my dear Non, and I want to tell it to you now.

There once was a woman who committed a terrible crime. She lived many years not remembering she had committed the crime. Then one day she was sent to prison and sent to die, and it was then that she remembered her crime. She was made to stand in front of a firing squad, but even after all the shots were fired, she was not gone. She had realized that death is not the end, it is just a cloud one walks through, and that when she walked out through the other side of the cloud, she would still be there and she would see everyone again, especially her daughter, whom she had always loved and whom she never had the chance to tell that she was sorry that she had committed the crime. Before she was shot, though, she wanted her daughter to know of her love for her and she wanted to ask the daughter for forgiveness and so she wrote a letter telling her these things, and telling her daughter to watch for her, for one day she would return and they would be together again.

When Mata Hari was finished, she sealed the letter. Clunet had arrived at the door of the prison to join her and her escorts on their way to the Caponnière, the field at the Palace of Vincennes, where Louis XVI and Marie Antoinette spent their last night. Please make sure Non gets this, she said to Clunet, and she was about to hand it to him when she thought better of it, seeing how his hands were all wet from the tears he was continually wiping from his eyes, and instead she opened up his jacket and slipped it into his breast pocket. As she did so, he kept saying that he was sorry, that he had tried to get her a pardon. He had tried, he said, and this time she noticed that even his nose seemed to be crying, as clear fluid ran from it and hung in a watery bead at the tip.

The cars they were in drove across the bumpy field of the Caponnière, where at one end was a stake, a limb of a young tree, stuck into the ground. The cars stopped and Mata Hari got out first. Then she turned and helped Sister Leonide out of the car.

There were twelve men in the firing squad. Six in front, and six behind, but not directly behind, centered in such a manner so that they were between the shoulders of those men who were in front so that their rifles had a clear path to the target.

Sister Leonide was saying, Mary, Mother of God, pray for us, now and at the hour of our death.

NO USE

IT WAS NO USE, thought Anna Lintjens, she could feel that the bills were slightly damp even after all the opening and closing of the neckline of her dress.

After the horse-drawn cab left her off at the entrance to the prison, she told the cabdriver to wait for her and then she walked up the stone steps and knocked on the door. Charles, who had not been assigned to the execution, rose from his chair at his desk and came to open it.

Yes? What is it? he said.

She did not know what to say, so instead she reached inside her dress and pulled out the damp roll of bills and put them on his desk.

What's this? Charles said.

It's a bribe, she said.

For what?

For Mata Hari.

Charles sat back down in the chair. He felt the cut on his Adam's apple beginning to bleed again and he pulled out his handkerchief and held it to his throat.

How much is there? he asked.

Anna Lintjens shrugged. A lot, she said, and while she said it the bills seemed to acknowledge what she was saying and began to unfurl, displaying the many heads of rulers on their sheets of well-worn paper.

Where did you get that kind of money, old lady?

Men. A lot of men, Anna Lintjens answered. Charles nodded, then he stood up, and he took the roll of francs, and he took Anna Lintjens by the arm, and he led her back outside to where her cab was waiting for her.

You're too late, he said.

Too late?

Charles looked at his watch. By five minutes, he said.

Anna Lintjens nodded her head. Then she turned and held out her hand so that Charles could place the roll of francs back in it.

Charles shook his head. This is what we call an illegal bribe of a prison officer, he said.

Anna Lintjens had to do it to the school bully once. She remembered how it worked. First you punch him where he's already hurting. In the case of the school bully it was in the black eye he already sported from a row with his father. Punching him there made him release the lunch money he had stolen from her at school. It spurted blood anew all over, and the dirt of the schoolyard quickly drank it up. In the case of Charles, it was of course his Adam's apple that was her target. To deliver the blow this time, her fist was not the instrument, but instead she used an extralong sewing pin she had placed in the bun at the top of her head before she set off on her trip. You never know when you might need a little protection when traveling in a strange place. The jab into his neck with the extralong pin brought Charles to his knees and he dropped the roll of francs and grabbed his throat with both hands, the same way the bully had dropped her lunch money and brought both of his hands to his black eye. Before Charles's blood could even begin to fall and stain the roll of francs and the stone of the Paris sidewalk, Anna Lintjens swiftly picked up the money and then she was off and inside the cab, which she had told to wait for her, just in case, of course, she had been lucky enough to make a quick getaway with Mata Hari.

In the horse-drawn cab, driving back to her hotel still holding the roll of francs, Anna Lintjens remembered what Mata Hari always said about plans. She always said that she hated them, that they either were wrecked, or foiled, or not carried out and Anna Lintjens had to agree with her about plans. Hers certainly never seemed to work out, and now the horse-drawn cab was moving slowly through the heart of Paris, a city Anna Lintjens had never visited before, and she could not see what was outside the window, the tears in her eyes were making everything, the buildings, the river, the bridges, just one blurred mix of a vision. And damn journeys, anyway, she thought, you never get to see all that you want to.

JUSTINE

IF YOU ARE about to be executed, don't accept the blindfold they give you to tie around your eyes. Shake your head no to the ropes they would use to tie around your hands and that they would use to tie your body to the stake made from the young tree limb thrust into the ground. Set your eyes on the nun who is crying for you and who is wearing your coat that you gave her because the morning is damp and chilly, and think to yourself how small she is and how big the coat looks on her small frame. Set your eyes also on the doctor who has taken care of you and whose trouser legs are brown from him kneeling in his garden tending to his radishes.

Do not set your eyes on the twelve soldiers of the Fourth Zouave Regiment. Do not listen to the Sabre à la main! they shout. The Présentez armes! they shout. Maybe you can't help it, though. Your eye catches the glint of a saber being raised in the sky by the officer of the men and you avert your eyes just for a moment from the nun and the doctor, long enough to see where you really are — in a field full of dead grass, swirled and matted, dry yellow blades by your fashionable button-up-the-ankle shoes.

When the call, Joue!, is shouted by the officer and he lowers his saber and the soldiers raise their rifles to their cheeks, smile, you are about to walk through the cloud that you thought for so long was a crushing wall of water.

AFTER SHE had fallen to the dry grass on the ground from the eleven shots (one Zouave, the twelfth Zouave, had been up all night concerned that he could not shoot a woman, could not bring himself to fire), her pearl gray dress ballooned up around her and a cavalry sergeant marched up to her to make sure she was dead and he fired the coup de grâce, a shot that went through her ear.

Dr. Bizard then had to determine that she was dead and he went up to her with his stethoscope in his ears and he unbuttoned the pearl buttons on her pearl gray dress front and he slid his stethoscope in and listened to her chest and when he heard nothing he pulled his stethoscope out and the sound receiver was covered in blood and he realized he had been trying to listen to her heart where instead there was a bullet hole.

No ONE claimed the body. The body was given to science, and one day a young medical student named Arboux walked into the dissection laboratory, and there, waiting for him on the metal table, was Mata Hari covered from head to toe in a sheet. When he lifted back the sheet he saw a female cadaver, approximate age forty-three, approximate height five feet ten inches, approximate weight 140 pounds. He named her Justine and set to work using a scalpel to peel off her skin, a job he bragged to his fellow students in the laboratory that was not as difficult as theirs considering there were eleven bullet holes in her body and therefore less skin to peel.

*　　*　　*

WHEN MACLEOD read the news of her death he was in the room of his favorite whore, Lise, who wore her dyed-red hair piled on her head, except for tendrils of it that looked as if the curly tails of pigs were hanging by her cheeks. He was waiting for Lise to finish whatever she was doing in the toilet so she could come to him. The paper was there on the rickety table by the bed and he was still reading the article when Lise came out of the toilet and knelt down in front of him and unbuttoned his fly and an image came back to MacLeod of Mata Hari standing in front of her mirror in their hut in Java and dancing with her arms out and the ends of her long black hair looked like the tips of black flames, only the flames weren't pointing upward, but downward, and he remembered thinking then an unclear thought of how she just might do it, she just might set the floorboards of the house on fire just with the ends of her hair.

SISTER LEONIDE kept Mata Hari's blue wool coat and she took it to the dressmaker and had the length of the sleeves shortened and had it taken in at the shoulders. She liked the coat, and every night, while she said her prayers before bed, she prayed for Mata Hari's soul and then she thanked Mata Hari again, for the coat kept her warm even on the coldest days.

DR. VANVOORT walked first on the windy palm grove trail, and his brown servant girl walked behind him. On her head she carried a basket filled with their babi and ayam nasi lunch wrapped in banana leaves and star and sukah and jackfruit and also newspapers that he had not yet read but were a few weeks behind, considering that was how long it took for the papers to make the trip from Holland to Java.

When he arrived at the white sand beach he looked out into the sea and saw the smooth gray backs of dolphins heading westward.

His brown servant girl removed her sarong and laid it on the fine sand and he lay belly down on the flowered cotton cloth and she opened the woven reed basket and gave him a newspaper and he started to read.

While he read, his brown servant girl massaged his muscles under the scapula of his shoulders, where he had always told her to, because it was there that the muscles tightened the most from picking the coffee beans from his plants all day long, and when he came to the article about Mata Hari being shot in front of a firing squad, he reached around and grabbed his brown servant girl's wrist and said, Tidak, and he pushed her away and so she stopped and waited for what he would tell her to do next.

While she sat there, a rare ajak trotted across the shoreline and she pointed to it and was about to call out, to tell Dr. VanVoort what she saw, but then she stopped herself, she knew he did not want to be disturbed at the moment, and so he never saw the rare ajak, and he died, many years later, never having seen one and never believing that his brown servant girl had either, because even the ajak's paw prints at the shoreline were quickly washed away by the incoming tide.

CLUNET had forgotten about the letter in his jacket pocket which Mata Hari wrote and had asked him to send to Non. He had worn his black jacket the day of Mata Hari's execution and it was a jacket he wore only on special occasions and to funerals and so it hung in his closet for a year and was only removed by his wife who gave it to the undertaker so that he could wear it the day of his own funeral. Clunet's wife, in her grief, had forgotten to check the pocket of the jacket and so she never found the letter, and it was buried with Clunet in his coffin in a cemetery in a lush valley of the Pyrenees known for its thermal waters that cater to the vocal cords. Opera singers, lawyers, and politicians hoarse from promises all gather in the valley to breathe in the healing vapors.

JUST LIKE MATA HARI

NON KNEW it was wrong, but she had done it anyway. She had entered the house through a window that was open a crack when she noticed that Anna Lintjens had not been home for days. She did not know Anna Lintjens had gone to Paris to save her mother, but she could tell by the fact that every time she walked by the house in the evening, and no lights were on, that the maid must be away. Anna Lintjens was like that about houses. She believed they needed to breathe and she always kept a window open no matter what the weather.

Non went straight to Mata Hari's room and she opened her closet and she put her face against the sleeves of her mother's dresses and breathed in the smell of her mother and then she tried on all of her mother's dresses and all of her shoes and even her elbow-length kid gloves and then she tried on her costumes, the silver headpieces embedded with cut glass made to look like real jewels and the wide armbands and the brassieres made of strung-together beads and decorated with pearls and garnets and lapis lazuli and moonstone.

An hour later, when she heard a noise in the street that might have been Anna Lintjens coming home, she quickly put the clothes and the costumes back, and when she returned to her aunt Louise's house her aunt Louise kissed her on the cheek and wondered what perfume Non was wearing and it reminded her of someone and it wasn't until the next morning, when Louise was working in her garden, making sure the bed of dirt where the tulip bulbs would come up in the spring was free of strangle weed, that Louise remembered. Mata Hari had smelled the same way.

Later, when Non read in the paper that her mother had been executed, she decided she would go back to Java someday. She wanted to find the house they lived in together. She had memories of sitting with her mother on a reed mat on the floor. She was telling Non not to move, she was busy weaving the small white bunga melati buds through her braids. You don't want the petals bruised, do you? she had said to Non. That was almost the only memory she had of her mother, she could not remember anything else.

A year later, Non graduated from nursing school and she accepted a job in Java. Her ship was supposed to set sail the next day when she felt a headache coming on. Louise said it was all the rushing around she had been doing. Why, every time she looked in the young woman's trunk Non had taken out a sensible dress that Louise had put in there.

It's not sensible, Non had told her aunt. I remember the heat, I was there, you weren't, she said. If I wore this dress in the heat I would die.

What then do you expect to wear while you're there, those vulgar sarongs like your mother wore? Aunt Louise said.

And then Non held onto one side of her trunk and turned it and tipped it over and emptied out all the clothes Aunt Louise had packed and said, Yes, that's exactly what I'll wear, I'll be just like my mother. I'll be just like Mata Hari.

Louise was about to yell at Non because the hasp shackle of the trunk, when it was turned over, scraped deep and painful-looking scratches into her just polished floorboards. But she didn't get a chance to yell. Non's headache became so terrible that she fell back onto the bed.

At the funeral Aunt Louise told MacLeod that there were no last words that Non spoke before the embolism struck, unless of course you count her saying, Yes, that's exactly what I'll wear, I'll be just like my mother. I'll be just like Mata Hari.

WHIRLPOOLS

THERE WERE enough francs to do it, Anna Lintjens thought. Enough francs to visit the town she grew up in and offer the old man farmer, who she found out was still alive, a down payment for one of the houses he had on his land. So she did it and moved into the house.

It was summer again, and the corn was at its highest when the farmer continued his tradition and cut another maze through the field right before harvest. An old lady in a long black skirt now, she walked through the maze along with children from the town. Their voices carried up over the ears of corn, the yellow tassels shuddering in a breeze or just from the sounds of the children's excited voices as they ran, shouting through the stalks. The gluey leaves dragged against the cloth of her skirt and the sleeves of her blouse, as if to grab her gently, wanting her to stay. She caught glimpses of the children as they ran. Seen through a space in the rows she saw their sun-streaked hair, their sun-browned arms as they pushed the stalks aside, trying to find a way out.

There were even enough francs left over for a horse. She had loved Mata Hari's horse, Radjah, and went to buy him back from the stable that Mata Hari had sold him to. In the stable she saw that he still had the look in his eyes that he had when Mata

Hari had come back from riding him and the look seemed to say that he had just galloped to the edge of the world and back. She knew she was too old to ride him, but she kept him and groomed him and held his shank and walked him on the roads, taking him to town with her when she ran her errands, talking to him as she walked, pointing out the bluebells and baby's breath that grew by the sides of the road. She was careful not to walk him too far, though, remembering how his hooves once suffered when Mata Hari rode him to find Non and how he needed to stand in buckets of ice in order to heal.

He nickered when she came to him in the field and trotted up to meet her at the fence. He had cowlicks on his neck by his mane, swirls like small whirlpools, and she thought if she looked at them long enough she could enter into him that way, become a part of him, the way a whirlpool made of water could take one down into the deep. On his shoulder there was an angel's kiss, a dimple in his chestnut hide that she often kissed when she first saw him or when she said good-bye.

At home she washed his blankets in a large metal tub, the salt from his body quickly clouding up the water. While she ate her meal alone she sometimes stopped bringing the fork to her mouth, and she would turn her head and lift her shoulder so she could smell the smell of Radjah on her sleeve. And sometimes, on a warm night, she would even bring her own blanket with her to the field and lay it down on the soft grass near where her horse stood and he would bend his head down to her before she fell asleep, his lips touching her ear or her smiling mouth.

A GOOD GHOST

IF YOU WANT to be a good ghost, stay quiet for almost a century. Then, on the anniversary of your death, begin to haunt the dreams of a writer so that the writer tells your story the way it should be told.

Signed,
Mata Hari

YANNICK MURPHY is the author of *Stories in Another Language, The Sea of Trees,* and *Here They Come.* The recipient of a Whiting Writers' Award, a National Endowment for the Arts fellowship, and an O. Henry Prize, she has also written a children's book, *Ahwoooooooo!* She lives in Reading, Vermont, with her husband and three children.